STO√

FRIENDS
OF ACPL

The Looking Glass Factor

The Looking Glass Factor

Judith M. Goldberger

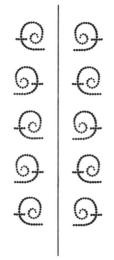

E. P. DUTTON   **NEW YORK**

Library of Congress Cataloging in Publication Data

Goldberger, Judith M.   The looking glass factor.
SUMMARY: A young girl and two feline friends continue the
research of a famous scientist who experimented with a
mental process known as merging.
        [1. Science fiction] I. Title.
    PZ7.G56444Lo 1979 [Fic] 79-11405
            ISBN: 0-525-34148-X

Published in the United States by E. P. Dutton, a Division
of Elsevier-Dutton Publishing Company, Inc., New York
        Published simultaneously in Canada by Clarke,
    Irwin & Company Limited, Toronto and Vancouver

    Editor: Ann Durell   Designer: Patricia Lowy
        Printed in the U.S.A.   First Edition
            10 9 8 7 6 5 4 3 2 1

for David, Benjie, and Anna—
where it all comes from
and where it all goes

my thanks to Agnes and Putney

A History of Earth

The year 2048 will go down in history alongside the most important of dates. It was the year when our foolish wasting of natural resources finally turned full in on itself. It was the year our planet nearly died, when Mother Earth declared a long-awaited war on us and we declared a Time of Terror.

After famine, blight . . . an almost total ravaging of things living, one cannot say too much or do too much. And so chaos reigned on Earth for more than fifty years.

Finally the remnants of the human race looked at

the remnants of everything else and began to think and to reorder. Survival became the key word in every aspect of living. Governments were headed by conservationists who dictated every move people made, every bit of energy spent.

Order returned; waste did not. It took three more centuries of rebuilding and rethinking before the dictators allowed people the luxury of investing energy in anything besides agriculture, population control, and resource development. Education, music, art, anthropology, and so many other areas of human endeavor began, at last, to be pulled from the archives, explored again. Scientists, too, took up nonsurvival research once more.

The year 2432 was another important one, though no one guessed it then. In a laboratory, a genetic mutation occurred in the fetuses of some ordinary house cats. The result was a new species, a race of intelligent beings.

Their struggle for a toehold in a totally human world was not easy. But it was inevitable. The Cat was something that could not be made light of for long. Sooner or later, humans had to see that they couldn't be gods, deciding who ruled the universe and who did not. That seeing was a big step toward becoming a truly mature race of thinkers. . . .

It is the year 2778. Together, human and Cat have learned much about life. They are about to learn even more. . . .

The Looking Glass Factor

1

Hannah Markus walked quickly toward her advisor's office. She knocked—once—on the door, then pushed it in.

In the middle of a bright yellow room, Fern Samelson sat before an enormous, cluttered desk, marking papers. To Hannah, Fern's pale, striped fur looked even more untidy than usual; her white whiskers twitched irregularly with concentration as she maneuvered the opposable writing device strapped to her paw. The pencil, held between Fern's paw pads and the opposable, made swift scratching sounds on the paper.

Hannah shuffled as noisily as she could. The Cat's head jerked up and her yellow green eyes focused on Hannah. She stood up and waved her tail broadly in greeting.

"When did you get in here? I didn't even hear you come." Fern Samelson's melodious voice conveyed fatigue. She sat down again and waited for Hannah to do the same.

Hannah seated herself, cross-legged, across the low desk from Fern.

"I'm sorry if I bothered you. . . ." She stared at the carpeting by her ankles and wished her advisor would say something, anything.

Fern Samelson slid the opposable from her wrist. "What is it, Hannah? The geometrics project? Are you snagged on some problem?"

"No," said Hannah. "That is, yes, but it's not a problem with the project." She shifted from side to side on the floor and twisted a strand of long, brown hair around and around her finger. "I want to go home today. I know it's only Monday. I can't wait till the weekend."

Fern ran a paw across her forehead. "Why?"

"Well, it's the Brancusis. They cabled me to come right away, but they didn't tell me why, so I can't tell *you*. It just sounded so important, because of the cable, you know." She released the coil of hair from around her finger. "I really want to go, but I guess I also don't want to. There's the project, and my writing course, and I was just beginning to work on a new set of skills in ESP. . . ."

"Well, Hannah," said Fern. "I can understand why you have mixed feelings. I'd be surprised if you didn't, considering the kind of student you are. But Agnes and Putney wouldn't call you away from school on a lark. I know them pretty well; they were my students once, too."

"Agnes and Putney don't go in for larks," Hannah said.

Fern Samelson blinked rapidly, then stared at her desk. "No," she said. "No, they don't. Still . . ." She looked up. "For some reason, the Brancusis have decided not to explain to either of us why they need you. Here is what I want from you, Hannah: Come right back if you think that what they're doing is not as important as what we're doing. I'll have to trust you to decide that."

Hannah stood up. "All right, Fern Samelson. I'll phone you as soon as I know how long I'll be gone."

"Don't forget to tell the other people on your project. You can extend the due date one week, but no more than that."

Hannah reached down to shake her advisor's paws.

Fern Samelson blinked uneasily. "For some reason, I feel I should be telling you to fare well." She took the girl's hand in her two paws and held it tightly for a moment.

The monorail car sped noiselessly toward the city, carrying Hannah with it. She watched the surface-level agrifields pass by, an endless checkerboard of soft-toned spring colors, but her mind was not on them. Her round, dark eyes stared uncaringly out the window as she twisted and twisted the hair strand around her finger.

Because of the Brancusis, Hannah was doing something that went against her grain like a rusty saw. In two years at Whole School, she had only once needed to leave in the middle of the week, to attend an important recital of her father's. A totally excusable, expected reason to upset your schedule. But this! Hannah twisted her hair tighter and faster. She didn't even know what the twins wanted her for.

Whatever it was, Hannah reasoned to herself, it must be important—especially if it had anything to do with why they had closeted themselves away for three weeks. In all that time, they hadn't budged out of Agnes' apartment. But was it important enough to have gotten her project partners mad at her about losing time? Important enough to miss even one day of school? Important enough to risk going straight to Agnes' apartment without stopping off at home? The more she thought about the risks she had taken, the more excitement and fear mingled in her and grew.

Well, she thought, it had better be that important. She tried imagining what it could all be about, but nothing came to mind. Most of what the Brancusis worked on was far too technical for her to understand. Hannah had no clues.

Suddenly, it seemed, the monorail had reached the outskirts of the city. That first sight always made Hannah feel like some kind of toy person. Hundred-story buildings rose up as one enormous, multicolored wall. The city's great clay-colored mountains pressed their immense weights against each other, pushed outward with silent force, drove themselves deep, deep, another hundred stories down into the earth. Each stood comfortable in the knowledge of its birthright: to destroy one nature and create a new one.

Hannah hummed a popular song.

The rivers of time wind around the city,
Between her great towers
And down to her roots.

It was easy to see where the songwriter had found his images.

The monorail car began making its stops, bumping softly as it ceased and then as it began its journey again. The doors swished open and shut a dozen different times. Finally, Bissell Street Station came into view. Hannah swung her small backpack over one shoulder, the car stopped, and she stepped out.

The early afternoon shopping crowds swept her along as she walked down Bissell Street. It felt strange to be in the city on a weekday, but no one seemed to notice a schoolgirl alone in the middle of the day.

Ten twenty-five Eastman Boulevard was a cylindrical building with a surface of smooth red clay. Built in the twenty-sixth century, it had some antique charm about it but was not without certain modern conveniences. It suited Agnes Brancusi well.

In the lobby, Hannah pressed a button and kneeled

down to speak into the intercom. "It's me, Agnes. I'm here."

Immediately she heard Putney's high, thin voice. "Come on up," he said, "but enter quietly."

Hannah straightened up and pushed the door open. A quick ride to the eighty-second floor and in a moment she was knocking softly at Agnes' door.

The door swung open and Putney Brancusi stood before Hannah, his paw raised to his mouth in a gesture commanding silence. Hannah tiptoed behind his sleekly furred black-and-white figure as he led the way to the narrow little kitchen.

"Come on, Putney. Tell me, tell me! It's really big, isn't it? Is it a secret? Is that why you . . ."

Putney turned slowly to face Hannah. "Please," he said with the calm of a Cat. "You will learn everything at the proper time. Meanwhile, I must insist that you not raise your voice."

"Oh, Putney," said Hannah. She took a deep breath, then let it out slowly. Putney waited. "You might at least give me some hints," she said then, quietly. "I don't see how you can go about things this way."

"What way?"

Hannah shrugged her shoulders. "You know—letting everything happen 'at the proper time,' even if I'm dying of curiosity."

"It is the way of Cats. While thinking, think. While walking, walk. The earth turns no faster when a person runs."

8

"Yes, yes, I know. I've heard that before." Hannah looked up suddenly. "If that's true, why did you send . . ."

"An urgent cable? Because it's nearly time. *Today* is the time. And there is nothing in your life that is more important than what is happening here and now."

So there was nothing to do but wait. Hannah sat down hard on the cool tiles of the kitchen floor. She felt, suddenly, tired and hungry at the same time. "Where's Agnes?"

Putney rose and peered around the door into the living room. "She's here. She's . . . busy." He turned to Hannah, who, still sitting, was reaching into the nearby refrigerator.

Hannah closed the refrigerator door, a dairy drink in her hand. She put the can to her lips and felt the cool liquid going down.

Putney shifted his narrow body from side to side, as if trying to choose a sitting position, but he remained on his feet. Now *he* seemed to be the nervous one.

"You're here in time to see the last of today's exper iments. Agnes should be about ready by now." He reached out and gently placed a paw on Hannah's knee. "Come," he said.

Hannah followed him out of the kitchen and into the living room, which was furnished sparsely with an exercise-climber; a large, ancient Oriental rug; and a few paintings. The curtains were drawn shut, but three small glow spots lit the room well. Agnes was nowhere in sight.

There seemed to be nothing to say or do; a heavy silence hung in the room. Hannah stood still and considered the lean figure of Putney, poised as if listening or perhaps smelling for something.

In a minute, Putney spoke, hushed and distant. "I can't prepare you for this, Hannah. I've had a hard enough time preparing myself during the last month. I'll say this, though. In the history of human and Cat, probably only three people have ever witnessed what you're going to see. I want you to see it now, and I want you to believe it. Because it is happening and it is real."

By instinct, Hannah turned away from Putney to follow the direction of his gaze; her eyes rested on a blank wall. But, no . . . it was not quite blank. And then she saw, but she neither believed nor didn't believe.

A dark spot, a bump, protruded from the center of that wall, about a meter up from the floor. It was only a centimeter wide. It had a rounded part and lighter, spiked part. Then, slowly, it grew. It became the small, fur-encircled toe of a Cat's paw. The toe expanded into a whole, white paw and then, flexing as if waking from sleep, groping and pushing out, it moved away from the wall.

Then suddenly, the paw lengthened into part of a long-haired leg, and from another spot along the wall, digits, a paw, and finally a matching front leg. They reached out, stretching toward the space before them, and all at once, straining with effort and gasping for breath, Agnes Brancusi came out of the wall.

She tumbled to the floor and lay there, exhausted and panting like a newborn animal, but Hannah made no move to help her. She watched mindlessly as Putney stood over Agnes, quietly licking her face and trunk.

In another minute, Agnes looked much better, still tired but not helpless. Then she saw Hannah and her face seemed to brighten up.

"What—is that real?" To Hannah, her own voice sounded cracked and gritty.

Agnes put her head back and let out the freest, most joyful Cat-laugh Hannah had ever heard.

"It's as real as can be!" she cried.

2

Hannah stood there for a long time, watching Agnes rearrange herself into a sitting position. Agnes still looked tired. Her full, brushlike tail lay at a skewed, abandoned angle, but her eyes were bright with excitement. Putney's eyes shone too as he stood over his sister.

I didn't see that, Hannah thought. But she knew she *had* seen it. She had watched Agnes go through a solid wall, as an ant might pass through a sand hill or a turtle push through a wall of mud. Suddenly Hannah too felt exhausted. She sat down heavily on the floor, unable to think any further.

It was quiet for a while. Putney turned his head toward Hannah and gazed questioningly at her. Do you see what we have done? he seemed to be saying.

Hannah closed her eyes. She didn't know why it was happening, but she could feel a familiar tightening in her throat. She thought she might cry.

When she opened her eyes again, Agnes and Putney were sitting together watching her, as calm as clams. She opened her mouth . . . and breathed through it. What she wanted to do most right then was scream. But Agnes and Putney would probably throw her out if she didn't act scientific about it.

What came out was something in-between. "How did you do it? Trick mirrors?" It sounded dumb even as she said it. This was not coming out right at all. She began feeling light-headed.

Putney looked at her with concern. "It must be much harder on her than we thought it would be, Agnes. It's too sudden."

"Yes. We should have introduced the idea slowly. Well, it's too late now. Are you all right, Hannah?"

"Sure, sure, I'm all right. Just tell me how you did that, will you?"

"It's called *merging*," Agnes told her. "It's very easy to explain and very hard to do."

"I bet. Do you have a machine or something to get you through?"

"No, dear. It's entirely a mental process."

"All *mental*? You mean to say that your mind opened up that wall and let you go through it?"

"No, no!" Agnes waved a paw at Hannah, dismiss-

13

ing the idea. "I didn't open the wall up; the wall opened itself up. Or rather, it let me inside."

"Inside?"

Agnes rolled onto the rug, extended her short legs, and propped herself up on an elbow. "I merged with the wall and then, when I wanted to leave, I un-merged, so to speak. Or, to be technical, I emerged. But the wall had to let me do it, you see, or I'd never have gotten in."

"Wait a minute!" Hannah shouted. "You're not trying to tell me that wall has a mind, too."

"She never said that, Hannah," Putney remarked quietly. "So, just let her finish explaining. It's not that the wall thinks, or anything like that. . . ."

"It just becomes receptive when it's been made aware of my wanting to get into it," said Agnes. "Strictly speaking, it isn't even telepathic. For that, you need two minds, and a wall hasn't got a mind. That's obvious." Agnes sighed, searching for a way to explain. "I suppose it's like sound waves. The wall feels vibrations coming from my mind and it reacts to them."

This was getting stranger by the minute. "So how come no one ever falls into a wall by accident?" Hannah asked.

"No one ever has or will—because it can't happen by accident. You have to want to merge badly, and you have to know exactly how to do it."

Putney took a deep breath and let it out again. "It took us many long hours of harnessing our mental powers in order to get this going. In fact, this is only the third time either of us has successfully completed a full merging."

"But what do you mean by *merging*? What is merging into what? Where did you find out about it?" Hannah asked, bewildered.

"Let me begin at the beginning," said Putney. "Have you ever heard of Margo Krupp?"

"No. Should I have?"

"Hmm . . . I guess not, not if you aren't in ESP research. She was a pioneer in her field, a remarkable human being."

"Was?" asked Hannah.

"She died about six weeks ago," said Agnes. "There was some sort of accident with a pressure lock on one of the earth-moon shuttles. She was lost in space. That's where the story starts, really."

A strange beginning, thought Hannah. What would the middle and end be like?

Now Putney spoke. "Margo Krupp was a close friend of Agnes'. They worked together on a psycho-kinesis project for the government a few years back. Anyway, Margo willed Agnes some of her research notes, and Agnes received them a couple of weeks after her death.

"Agnes took the notes home and read through them nonstop. Then she called me. I sat up overnight and read what amounted to a chronicle of eight years of intensive research. Clinical research." Putney stared past Hannah.

"The idea seemed impossible to execute, but we kept on reading and rereading until we had to admit it: Margo Krupp must actually have done the thing she worked toward those eight long years."

"Margo had worked out a method for achieving a physical impossibility," said Agnes.

"No, you shouldn't say that," Putney cautioned her. "Humans in flight was once a physical impossibility; universal environmental balance seemed like a physical impossibility, too. So was a cure for cancer, come to think of it." Putney shook his head. "Maybe nothing is impossible. . . ."

"In any case," said Agnes, "Doctor Krupp kept those notes locked up in a safe-deposit box, and for good reason. Her discovery raises frightening questions about power—in the right places and in the wrong places. As far as we know, she was the only person who participated in the work recorded in the books. So now Putney and I are party to her research. We decided, for various reasons, to include you too."

So, they were telling her these secret things for a purpose, thought Hannah. But what purpose? Why?

"The long and the short of it," continued Agnes, "is that we decided we had to prove to ourselves that Margo could have done what she said she had done— by doing it ourselves. We wanted to prove this before we told anyone, even you, Hannah. Because if we were involved in some bizarre hoax, or were following the ravings of a madwoman, we weren't going to be called anybody's fools."

"But you're *not* fools!" cried Hannah.

"Nevertheless," Agnes said, "our work these last few weeks was bound to go in one of only two directions: up in an idiotic whiff of smoke, or out, far beyond our wildest imaginations."

"And it went the second way, didn't it?" asked Hannah.

Putney and Agnes both nodded.

"All right," said Hannah. "How do you do it?"

"Well," said Agnes, "physically, I suppose, my molecules gradually suspend themselves, distribute themselves throughout the entire wall, and get mixed up with the wall's molecules. That's how I get in physically, although I haven't really thought about the physical aspects that much. Up till now, we've only been concerned with making it work. And making it work doesn't seem to be physical at all."

Not physical? But where had Agnes' body *really* been when she was all mixed up inside that wall? Bodies just didn't disappear or fall apart. Agnes seemed to be saying that they *did*.

"All right," Hannah said, "you go into this wall. Well, what happens then? How do you get out?"

"Physically," said Agnes, "I make my molecules reform themselves in a forward-moving direction; as they come together, they simultaneously move out of the wall."

So, that was the whole picture, more or less. Suddenly, impossible images started popping into Hannah's head: people walking through buildings, falling through floors; crowds moving in and out of places,

17

all at the same time, through doors, walls, and windows; *herself* passing through the walls of her apartment; her parents fainting when they saw her coming through the front door without opening it. Her parents! What time was it?

As if in answer to that thought, the phone rang. Agnes rose. She pushed the reply button on the wall and spoke her familiar cheerful greeting. "Hello! Doctor Brancusi here."

From the receiver grid, an equally familiar but irritated human voice spoke. "Doctor Brancusi, is my daughter there?"

"Absolutely, Abraham. How did you guess?"

"I didn't. Hannah?"

Hannah got up and came closer to the receiver grid. "Hello, Father. I didn't have time to call you before I left school."

Her father's voice rose ominously. "Why? What is the meaning of this? I called the school and they told me you had left in the morning. I had to locate your advisor to find out where you had gone. It's two o'clock now, Hannah."

She knew there were no answers to satisfy him.

"I'm sorry," she said weakly.

"Sorry! Is that all you can say? Really, Hannah, it seems quite obvious that I should know where you are at all times, without having to search for you. I've never known you to do anything like this before. Why aren't you in school?"

Hannah opened her mouth and saw Agnes and

Putney violently shaking their heads. "Uh . . . I had to see the Brancusis about their new telepathy project. They need to try something out on me and it can't wait. . . . It's very complicated."

There was a short silence, followed by "Well, see that you call me when you get back to school tonight."

"OK, Father. But why did you call me at school in the first place?"

Hannah's father sounded tired suddenly. "Oh, it was about the concert this Saturday. I wanted to be sure you remembered not to make any other plans for the day."

"I remembered. The Museum Hall. Two o'clock."

"Yes. All right, then. I must go to the rehearsal now. And Hannah . . ."

"Yes?"

"Please don't disappoint me like this again."

"No, I won't. Bye."

"Good-bye." The receiver clicked off. Hannah looked at her friends. "Well, it seems as if I'll be going back to school tonight."

Agnes twisted around to nip at a spot on her back. "How bothersome," she said, straightening up again. "But, for Abraham's sake, and for keeping a low profile, it's probably best that you do."

"That *is* bothersome," said Putney. "Now that you're involved, I feel as if you should be with us all the time."

"Wait a minute," Hannah said. "What do you

mean by *involved*? Why *am* I here anyway? Why do you need me?"

A momentary glance passed between the two Cats.

"We want you to work with us," said Putney. "There is so much to learn, so many questions that have to be answered."

Hannah felt a strange tightness rising up from somewhere in her intestines. The tightness reached her stomach and made it growl.

"But I'm just a kid," she said. "Why not some of your scientist friends?"

"Hannah," said Agnes, "we need you because you are the only person who can do the job."

"The only one?"

"The only one. First of all, we need a human being to help us, not another Cat."

"Why?" Hannah asked. "Why a human being?"

"Because Margo Krupp was a human being. There may be ways her mind and body reacted to the merging process that were different from feline kinds of reactions. Putney and I can't learn enough about merging just on our own.

"Secondly," said Agnes, "we must maintain absolute secrecy during our research. The idea of merging will have to wait to be unleashed in the world. Merging is a tremendous power, a dangerous power. No one else must know of it until we can learn more about what it is and what it can do.

"You are someone we know we can trust. That's not so easy to find, in case you didn't know." Agnes cocked her head sideways and looked at Hannah.

Hannah fidgeted. "All right," she said. "You trust me and I'm a human being. I can't be the only person you know who meets those qualifications. So *why me*?"

"Because," said Putney, "you also have one of the prime ingredients for making merging work."

"Oh? And what prime ingredient is that?"

"Hannah," said Agnes, "don't be thickheaded! How did we come to be friends? What drew us together in the first place?"

This is silly, thought Hannah. "We met on the government telepathy project."

"And what were you doing there?" Agnes prompted.

"I'm a Class 8 psychic and they wanted to use my . . . hey! I'm a psychic." She wrinkled her forehead in confusion. "So what?"

"Margo Krupp was too. A talented one, a Class 3," Putney replied. "She was convinced that her psychic powers were crucial to the development of her merging powers. The two seem to be very closely related."

Hannah waved her arms around. "All the Cats in the whole blasted world have *some* psychic powers. Human beings hardly ever have any. And I'm not even much of a psychic, either. All I can do is a little gross telepathy."

"We're Class 8s, too, Hannah, as you know," said Putney.

"But why did you single me out? Why me?"

"Because you *are* human! And because we trust you. We've already been through that!" cried Agnes.

So. There it was. Hannah had been drafted into service, and now it was obvious why she alone could help them.

"I won't do it."

Silence filled the room. The two Cats stared back at Hannah.

"I won't do it," Hannah repeated, backing toward the door. "I'm too young to get involved in something like this. I have to go back to school. And anyway"— she paused—"*it's too damned weird and scary!*"

She had reached the door by now and in one movement pushed it open and fled toward the elevator, away from her horrifying thoughts, back to the safety of school.

3

But she couldn't escape her thoughts. As she sat in the monorail car, a mental image seared Hannah's mind again and again: the picture of that paw protruding from the wall, slowly growing, becoming Agnes Brancusi. She kept trying to think of other things, but that image intruded. She lived the scene through and through until her mind felt crowded with it and an almost physical pressure started at the back of her head.

What did she need this for? She had enough headaches from school. The trip back seemed a long one.

It was beginning to get dark when Hannah left the

monorail station. Out among the sprawling agrifields, the school building rose fat and monumental, twenty-two stories high, its lights faintly illuminating the dusky, shrouded area around it. The Whole School was like some huge, clumsy beacon, lighting the way across a dim, quiet ocean, deserted but for one tired traveler.

Hannah scanned the top floor but saw no lights on in her living quarters. Her roommates must be eating dinner.

She glanced at her watch. Six-thirty! Dinner was just about over. They must all be in the library or else underground in the gyms. That gave her a chance to get settled before people started asking questions. She was far too tired to start inventing stories about her absence. Hannah used a side door, avoiding the huge, open lobby, and got into the freight elevator.

The hallway on the twenty-second floor was deserted. Between dinner and bedtime almost no one ever came back to those cramped sleeping rooms. Hannah turned in at the third door on the right, with the number 7 written on it.

The room she shared with nine others, Cats and humans, looked like every other sleeping room at Whole School: The Cats' mats, rolled up and stacked together at the far end of the room; five bunk compartments for the humans built into the wall, their doors slid shut. Against the opposite wall, pegs and built-in drawers for clothing and personal items, a sink with a row of toothbrushes along the top, and a toilet hidden inside its tiny cubicle. There was not much room for luxuries here; the lack of space kept everyone from collecting more possessions than he or she could care about.

Hannah hung her backpack on the peg labeled H. M. Wearily she pulled off her boots. There was no place soft and yielding to sit down on unless she used one of the Cats' mats. But people tended to have respect for the few places each could truly call his or her own, so Hannah hesitated. Then she remembered the call she had to make to her father. Bootless, she left the room.

At the end of the hall, a recessed hole held the telephone. Hannah sat down on the seat below it and pushed a button for the operator.

"School operator. May I help you?" said a mechanical voice.

"This is Hannah Markus," Hannah told the computer. "Please charge this call to my account. It's number 81-41-088." She gave her home number, then sat back and waited.

"Hello?" a mild, uncertain voice said.

"Hi, Mom. I'm back at school."

"Oh, hi, Hannah. It's good to hear from you. Your father said you had him quite worried. I was out all day."

Somehow Hannah got the feeling her mother was trying to sound more concerned than she in fact had been. In a funny way, it made her feel she had been trusted to do right, in spite of not having checked with them.

"Yes, well, I'm just calling to tell you I'm back at school. I don't have to talk to Father, do I?"

"He's rehearsing at the hall now, anyway. I'll tell him you called. And we'll see you Friday."

"Right, bye." Hannah stood up.

"Oh, Hannah? I almost forgot. Do you mind wearing your long dress to the recital on Saturday? It would make your father so happy."

"No, I don't mind," she answered. "You know I like that dress. Sometimes I need an excuse to get out of my coveralls, anyway."

Her mother laughed. "Me too, actually. Well, see you soon, dear."

Hannah repeated her good-bye and heard her mother click off the phone. She pushed the Off button. All of a sudden a rush of fatigue came over her. It felt like 2 A.M. instead of early evening.

Hannah walked slowly back to her room. She shed her coveralls, piled them into her drawer, and dragged herself up the ladder to the top bunk compartment. Then she slid open the door and fell into bed. "I'll just take a nap," she mumbled, "and then work on geometrics. . . ."

Voices beneath her made Hannah stir out of a deep sleep. At first she heard only rising and falling tones: There were complaining voices—one of them seemed very angry—and then a calm one that answered the others.

The voices began sounding familiar as she rose to the surface of consciousness. With a shock, Hannah realized that she was hearing a conversation about herself. She lay there in the dark, narrow sleeping cell and listened.

"I don't care!" the angry voice was saying. It belonged to Margaret Standish, a Cat who was one of Hannah's roommates and also a project partner. "The geometrics project was supposed to be my tour de force. I *still* say she's got nerve running out on us at practically the last minute."

"She might have called Fern today. Just to give us *some* idea of when she'd be back. It's immature, if you ask me." This was spoken bitterly by Margaret's best friend, Grace Horwich, another project partner, whose room was down the hall. Hannah could imagine their slim backs curving in stiff, reproachful sitting postures.

"Come off it, guys." The defending voice was Susan's! "We've all had to leave school in the middle of a project before. In fact, Hannah's been better about that kind of thing than anybody I know."

Good old Susan. It wasn't easy standing up to those two self-centered felines alone. Go to it, Hannah shouted at Susan through her mind. But Susan wasn't psychic—Hannah knew she wouldn't receive the message. She really ought to climb down and tell those Cats where to go.

"Everyone needs a break sometime," Susan was saying. "Even Hannah the Grind."

"Oh, hell! You mean she's taking time off now to play? At the very end of my star project?" Margaret's voice was getting shrill and thin.

"*Your* star project, is it? Since when is a project the special baby of one person?"

"Don't be stupid, Susan. All of this communal-effort garbage is just a cover, anyway. We're graded for individual performance."

"Communal work is the essence of Whole School!" yelled Susan. "Group effort! Cooperation! It forms a model for real life."

"Bung!" said Grace. "I just want good grades."

"Then what in the moon's name are you doing here? Go to Step School and leave the rest of us alone!"

A deadly silence filled the air. The three of them were obviously glaring at each other, waiting to see who would make the next move. Hannah could feel the tension rising up from the lower half of the room like heat.

It was her fight too, of course, and she ought to be down there with Susan. But something made her lie still. Wait, said a small, selfish voice inside her. Wait and see what else they say about you.

Margaret's voice, cold and controlled, pierced the quiet. "I am here, Susan, and I want to do well. I am here and Hannah Markus isn't. She is on her way to ruining a good thing. There's nothing you can say to make it better, either."

"I'm not trying to make it better," Susan said slowly. "I'm trying to tell you that anything Hannah does she does for a good reason. She would never have left on a silly whim."

"Then why *did* she leave?" asked Grace.

"I don't know. School is the most important thing in her life. I really don't know." Her voice trailed off weakly. Poor Susan. She had done her best.

"Drat her! Drat Hannah Markus! A whole project, a full third of a year's work, delayed and maybe even downgraded because of her. Come on, Grace. Let's go get a cup of tea." The door slammed shut.

Hannah heard Susan sigh. She would talk to her friend, tell her what had happened that day, explain that everything was all right again. She swung her feet out of the doorway of her sleeping cell and bent forward to climb down from her sleeping cell.

But suddenly Hannah knew that everything was not all right. She had listened to the argument, all that squabbling, with growing anger. And then, in the middle of it, her anger had died away and part of her was back in Agnes' living room, hearing the Brancusis' plea for help: "We want you to work with us. . . . There is so much to learn. . . ."

And then it came to her, as she sat on the edge of her cell. It hit like a painful blow to the face: What were school projects and these petty fights and slaving for grades when balanced against the discovery of Margo Krupp?

There was only one answer Hannah could give herself. It welled up inside her, shrinking her fears. Nothing! They're nothing! she wanted to shout. I'm going to be a part of that scary, incredible thing. I want to make it happen!

Quickly she climbed down the ladder.

"Oh! Hannah! What are you doing here?"

Hannah grabbed her friend by the shoulders.

"Susan, thanks for sticking up for me. I'm going away now. Look, will you cover for me? If anybody asks, you haven't seen me. I'm not back yet from the city. Don't tell Fern or anybody." She yanked her backpack off the wall and started pulling on her boots.

"Hannah, what's going on? When did you get here? What on earth are you going to do?" She pulled Hannah to her. "Are you in trouble or something?"

"No, no, I'm not. I have to get back to the city, that's all. Trust me." She swung the backpack onto her shoulders. "Listen, put off my parents if they call, will you? Tell them I'm on the toilet or something."

"Sure, sure."

"I don't know when I'll be back," Hannah said from the doorway. "A few days or . . . look, I don't know. Just do it for me, huh?"

Susan nodded as Hannah disappeared from the doorway. Even before Susan had wandered out of the room toward the library, her friend was trudging between shadowed fields back toward the monorail.

4

Sunlight streaked into the living room between half-closed slatted blinds, making Hannah cover her eyes with her arm. She rolled from her back to her stomach and slowly opened her eyes. She studied the pattern of Agnes' rug: the intricate paths of deep red, cream, gold, and black; the way the light hit it, making it look new; the way it looked old in the shadows. She ran her fingers lightly across one complicated little network of color and pretended that her hand was receding, slowly melting into the rug, merging with its tiny threads, strands that had lain full and new hundreds of years ago and been trodden by people who had never even dreamed of her world. Hannah lay there for a long time, letting her thoughts take her, tracing the designs of the rug.

By nine o'clock, breakfast was over. Three people sat in the uncluttered living room, preparing themselves for a work session.

Hannah, still in her rumpled coveralls from the day before, sat cross-legged, combing the night's tangles out of her hair. She felt remarkably refreshed, in spite of the previous day's commotion and the brief sleep on the floor of Agnes' apartment. She could feel energy pouring from her center out to her limbs, and this somehow made her feel older, more capable.

Putney sat statuesque in spite of himself, sleek and fine-boned, his black-and-white body curving precisely and ending in four carefully aligned paws. He stared out the window, waiting for things to begin.

His sister sat in a similar pose, reading from notes on the floor in front of her. Agnes' squat body contrasted with her brother's slim one. Her black-and-white fur billowed out uncontrollably, making her look broader than she really was. For several minutes her yellow eyes darted back and forth across the pages at her feet. Then she looked up and spoke in a businesslike manner.

"First of all, Hannah will need to get caught up on our work to date."

"Why don't I just read the notes?" Hannah suggested.

Agnes shook her head. "No, that will take too long, and it's too technical for someone not in the ESP field. I suggest we fill you in by talking and moving you through the whole process. It'll be a sort of practical indoctrination. Even that may take weeks, depending on your capabilities."

Hannah put her comb down. "You mean you're going to start teaching me to merge? Right now?"

Agnes looked at her brother. "I don't see why not," she said. Putney did not reply.

Hannah felt the fears of the day before crowd in around her, but she fought them, hard. You got this far, she told herself fiercely. Everything really important is scary. Her father had said that once! Then, with that stern man's imagined gaze of approval on her, Hannah felt far less afraid. She sat up straight and waited to hear about the next step.

Putney and Agnes were having a close, muffled conversation. Now Putney turned toward Hannah.

"We were just discussing how to begin with you," he said, sounding vaguely apologetic. Were they going to start talking down to her, Hannah wondered.

Agnes rose and gestured toward the window. "Hannah, come over here with me." Hannah followed her. They looked far, far down to the little street, with its stingy-looking patches of green mixed in like dirt specks in snow. Their gaze traveled up to the unbroken ranks of towering apartments. Above, the eternally huge sky opened to their view.

"Can you imagine yourself," Agnes said to Hannah, "as part of what you're seeing, with no physical boundaries separating you from anything?"

Hannah looked at her. Was she hearing Agnes right?

The Cat went on. "It's very important that you begin by letting go of the sense of yourself as a physically independent object. You are part of it all. There is nothing—neither flesh nor bones—that can hold you back, You're everything, Hannah, and it is you."

Hannah shuddered. Why was Agnes talking to her this way? It was so crazy! But she remained quiet, watchful.

"Now," Agnes said. "I want you to sit down again. Close your eyes and concentrate on what I'm telling you. That's it. Just relax and think about being part of everything around you. There are no boundaries. You are free. Just feel yourself expanding. . . ."

Slowly Hannah stopped fighting and wondering. As Agnes talked, she began following her instructions. Gradually she started to feel what Agnes was describing: Her limbs floating away. Her body expanding freely. A new sense of airiness coming in to take the place of the weight of her body. It was wonderful, like being in a gravity-free place and yet anchored somehow. She opened her eyes to see if anything looked different around her.

Instantly the feelings faded. Hannah had shriveled up into her old, heavy body. She almost felt like crying.

"Don't worry," Agnes said, rushing over to her and

patting her shoulder. "You were great—I could tell you were getting it. I never expected it to happen so fast."

"But it's gone!" Hannah looked around.

"You can make it come again. We'll work on it together, and in no time you'll be able to do it at will."

"Agnes?"

"Hm?"

"What does this have to do with . . ." Suddenly Hannah knew. "Boundaries!" she shouted. "We learn to get rid of them. Then they don't hold us in, and they don't hold us out!"

"That's right," said Putney.

"Right," said Agnes. "Only the feeling has to get stronger, much stronger, before you can begin to utilize it in the merging process. And there are quite a few other mental steps to take."

"Well, let's go," said Hannah, her eyes shining.

"We picked the right colleague, Doctor Brancusi," said Agnes.

"We certainly did, Doctor Brancusi." Putney sent up a deep-throated purr for emphasis.

They kept at it for most of that day—Hannah concentrating, Agnes talking. By evening they were all exhausted, but Hannah found that if she opened her eyes very slowly, she could keep the boundaryless sensation and look around, too.

After dinner, refreshed, they attempted to work

still more movement in. Hannah first tried raising her hand, then one arm, then both arms, and gradually her whole body. She stood, testing her fresh new self against the firm, real contours of her body. It took all her concentration to hold both awarenesses in mind at the same time: She was in her body, but she was also untied from it.

She told Agnes and Putney about it.

"Soon," said Agnes in reply, "we will teach you not to constantly need to check on your body. Then you can move around without having to keep two contradictory ideas in your head at the same time. It'll be a lot easier. You'll see."

They worked all day Wednesday. On Thursday morning, Hannah called Fern Samelson and told her, plainly, that what the Brancusis were dealing with was indeed more important than what she, Hannah, was doing in school.

"I won't argue with you" was her advisor's reply. "I want to see you back in school Monday morning, though."

Hannah couldn't argue either. Fern Samelson had been more than fair. She would have to reckon with her project partners eventually anyway. Not to mention her parents.

It would never do to keep her mother and father totally in the dark. It was an awful feeling, staying secretly with the Cats after she'd promised her father he would always know where she was. He'd almost certainly let her return to the Brancusis but only on weekends, and she would have to spend those evenings and nights at home, too. She knew she couldn't hope for more. Fortunately, the school year was coming to an end.

Three more weeks of this, thought Hannah, and then I'll work out something much better. It was the first time she could ever remember wanting school to be out of her life.

By Friday, Hannah was moving freely about Agnes' apartment, feeling only airiness and a sense of harmony with the things around her. This was part of the boundaryless state of mind. It took great concentration to get there, but once she had done it, the perfect pleasure of it took over and made Hannah feel that it was almost like play. Agnes and Putney followed her from room to room, calculating her progress, speaking encouraging and helpful words when they saw her waver.

Lunch that day began somberly, with feelings of good-bye. They all knew Hannah would have to go home that night. The Brancusis sat before the low dinner table, muttering about how much there was to do, how Hannah had only scratched the surface. She couldn't begin to participate in the research until she had at least learned the basics of merging. Apparently, thought Hannah, they had not reckoned with the obligations children normally have to other people. Research scientists seemed to work totally on their own, but children certainly did not.

"Well, why don't we just try to speed things up a bit?" Hannah asked, munching on a piece of bread.

Putney looked up from his bowl and carefully

cleaned a morsel of meat from his whiskers. "You're going fast enough as it is, in my opinion."

"Let me try," said Hannah. "If it doesn't work, we'll go back to where we are now."

Agnes swallowed. "I think she's right, Putney. We could try her on some partial mergings this afternoon. Then if . . ."

"It's foolish," Putney said. "You just can't rush these things."

Agnes bent over and took another bite from the mound in her bowl. "How do *you* know? How does anyone know?"

Putney stood up. "Don't be silly, Agnes," he said. "I *feel* that it's wrong. I've learned to merge and I know it's a delicate matter. Remember the time you panicked, in the very beginning? You had your head in . . ."

"All right. Let's not bring up messy matters now. You don't want to frighten our star pupil." Agnes rose and pushed her bowl toward Hannah. "Hannah, would you mind clearing these away?"

Hannah picked up the dishes without comment. She felt small and insignificant. She kneeled by the sink, washing the Cats' bowls and her own plate and silverware, and tried to make sense of the pieces of muffled dialogue coming from the next room. She couldn't hear much but she knew what the drift was. And she knew how to put a stop to it.

The Brancusis turned toward Hannah as she stepped into the living room.

"I want to get started," she said slowly and very deliberately. Putney opened his mouth, and closed it.

"I'll get the notes," said Agnes.

"All right then, *you* are without boundaries. Do you know that this wall is, too?"

Hannah stood by the blank wall in the living room with her eyes closed and her hand resting lightly against the wall's cool surface. She was trying to sense the wall in a new way. She began imagining that it was made of some soft, yielding material like mud or pudding.

"The wall is just like you, Hannah," Agnes was saying. "Just like you—flexible, without constraints, at one with everything else."

The pudding image faded. Hannah couldn't think of herself that way, no matter how boundaryless she felt. Air, she thought, it's all like air. I am like the wall; the wall is like me. I *am* the wall and it is me.

Slowly, so slowly, she pressed her hand forward against the wall. She felt its flatness fading, she felt nothing against her palm. She moved her hand forward some more. Still nothing! There was no pressure, not even coolness, only space. She felt she had to watch to see what it looked like.

She opened her eyes, and four things happened in rapid succession. First, Hannah saw the stump of her arm, ending with her wrist, flush against the wall. My hand! she thought, terrified. It's gone! Instantly her hand shot out from the wall, like the pole of a magnet held against an identical pole. And then, Hannah retched. All over the floor.

After she had gotten herself cleaned up and had sipped a cup of tea, the Brancusis explained what had happened.

"It's a terrible shock to realize that it's actually happening to you," Agnes told her. "It's really not possible to be fully prepared for the assault on your sense of self."

"Why was that an assault on my sense of self?" Hannah asked, befuddled.

"Because your first impression was that part of you was gone." Agnes' eyes winked at her in a Cat-smile. "One gets very attached to the parts of one's body."

"You quite naturally resisted the idea of losing your hand. And when it looked as if that had happened, you stopped accepting the relationship between the wall and you. The process stopped at that moment because you wanted it to."

Hannah rotated her empty mug in her hands. "It's sort of like learning to trust, isn't it? I mean, you have to feel that the wall will take care of your hand and will give it back, too."

"It *is* that, and it's more," said Putney. "The trusting goes further. In a way, you are becoming the wall. You're combining your molecules with its molecules. When you enter a wall entirely, you have to learn that you are still you, still a being, even though you have no tangible body. If you don't have faith in the existence of *you* as a person, with or without a body, merging doesn't work. And so you are learning to trust *yourself* in the end. That's the hardest thing of all to do."

Hannah could only sit still and try to take it all in. "I don't see how I'll ever get to that point," she murmured.

"You will," Agnes replied. "Faster than you know. Hannah, you have now *merged*. You've done what only a handful of people have ever done."

"With you, I did it."

"No, alone."

Hannah knew it was true.

5

A light in the third-floor apartment winked on just as Hannah approached the door of her building. She had timed things perfectly. She would arrive home at 5:45, precisely when she always returned from school on Fridays.

Hannah took the stairs to her floor—it was the one advantage she could think of to living this close to ground level: You had a choice of riding or walking. Once, just after her family had moved in, she had complained about living on the third floor. "There's no view here; I feel cramped in by buildings."

"Just be glad we're not subground" was all her mother had said in reply. It was enough for Hannah.

The building was a newish one and Hannah's apartment was very modern. Her mother had always wanted a sort of "This is it: the last word in a place to live" place. They had bid for a space in the building and had waited three years to get it. Still, after four years of living there, Hannah could not walk into the main room without sensing its ungainliness.

The room where the Markuses did all their eating and entertaining and most of their working was large and open. A huge panorama window at the far end of the room bulged outward like a balloon. The kitchen-dining area (Hannah called it the Pit) was recessed in the floor and was intended to appear to nestle in the window by virtue of its being circular. Kitchen appliances and cabinets in turn nestled in the walls of the recess. A large, round table did its nestling job in the middle of the recess. The rest of the room was squared off and allowed enough space for a piano, tape and bookshelves, and a few floor cushions. There was a bedroom on either side of the main room, and a bathroom on Hannah's parents' side. It was all maximum efficient, minimum friendly, Hannah felt.

Hannah's mother straightened up from the stove just as her daughter walked in. She smiled as she pushed short brown hair off her forehead. An older version of Hannah, wearing similar sturdy coveralls, her mother spoke softly.

"There you are. It seems like a long time, doesn't it?"

"It certainly does," replied Hannah. Her mother would never know just *how* long.

"Your father's taking a shower. He'll be out soon, I expect."

Hannah jumped into the Pit and kissed her mother on the cheek. "What's for dinner?" she asked.

"Just stew," said her mother. "And please remember to use the steps. You look like an ape when you go leaping about like that."

"Mmmm," said Hannah through a mouthful of stolen dinner roll. She sat down at the table and propped her feet up on the nearby steps leading into the Pit.

"Your cousins from Brewrist nearly stopped in for the evening," said Hannah's mother, stirring the stew.

"Mm, why didn't they?" Hannah turned to look at her mother.

"You know perfectly well why not. And they should know, too. Your father never has visitors the night before a recital. It's too distracting, and he needs to practice."

Hannah turned away. It was true, she did know. And it was useless to argue about such things.

"Where's Meor, anyway?" Hannah asked, scanning the room for their pet cat.

"Hello! Hello!" came a buoyant call from across the room. Hannah's father stood at his bedroom door, looking newly scrubbed. He had tied his kinky black hair back in a ponytail to keep it out of the way. He wore a long, purple gown, and with his arms spread wide in welcome and his teeth flashing, he looked like some messenger of a new faith. Meor twined around his ankles, rubbing tabby fur against the purple robe. Hannah couldn't help smiling. She jumped out of the Pit, picked up the purring cat, and stretched up to kiss her father.

"Hello to you!" she said. "How is the program going?"

"Can't you tell?" her father answered, beaming. Then, looking more severe, "You are through with this monkey business, yes?"

Hannah stroked Meor. "Oh yes. That is, I still need to see the Brancusis but only on weekends. And then . . ."

"Not this weekend, I trust."

"No, not this weekend. But, well . . ." She fought hard against the urge to tell her father a lot more. "It's something important. I want to keep working on it with Agnes and Putney this summer."

Her father looked deep into Hannah's eyes for a moment. It made her feel hot and fidgety but she stood her ground. The moment dragged on.

"As long as this 'important something' does not interfere with your schoolwork, or with your music lessons later on. Remember, you will be beginning piano study once again this summer."

"I know, Father," Hannah answered, relieved.

"And I *want* to start piano lessons again. I really think I'm old enough to appreciate it now."

"Well, good," her father said, giving her a squeeze. "That is the most important thing of all—that you enjoy music as much as is possible. He sighed. "For me, I enjoy it by immersing myself in it, by playing the compositions of the great masters, and by working my fingers to the bone. You, my daughter, will find your own way."

"I hope so," Hannah said. "It isn't going to be easy, I think."

"Nothing really good ever is," her father replied. "Come, let's have dinner and also a happy weekend together. And whatever it is you are doing with the Brancusis that takes so much of your mind off of other things, I hope that it is worth it to you."

Hannah smiled as gratitude welled up inside her. It was mixed with relief; obviously, her mother and father believed she had been at school since Monday night.

Even plain potato stew and salad could be wonderfully pleasant now that the tensions brought on by Hannah's adventure had been dealt with as openly as was possible. The sweet-tasting potatoes were still a little crunchy and did mix nicely with pine nuts. Over sesame candy and fruit, the Markuses discussed the acoustics of the recital hall, the party that would follow at their apartment, and what critics, if any, would be present to hear the program.

"Father," said Hannah, munching her last piece of

fruit after the talk had died down. "Do you think it's sad that Cats can't be musicians? I mean, that no one ever invented an opposable good enough to allow them to play real musical instruments?"

Her father stopped eating and sat looking out the window a moment. "No," he said at last. "In the first place, most of the computerized instruments—not 'real ones,' as you would call them—are available to Cats. They don't make much use of them. But, primarily, I doubt that Cats could be good musicians, even if they had the dexterity to play noncomputerized instruments."

"But lots of Cats appreciate music," Hannah countered.

"They do," replied her father. "But only from the outside looking in, so to speak. Appreciating is one thing; being a part of creation is quite another. Music is essentially a human thing, born of a special human kind of creativity. There almost seems to be a reason for Cats to be made with no physical ability to play musical instruments. They don't need it." He gave a short laugh. "Goodness knows there are enough bad musicians among us human beings."

Hannah's mother looked genuinely surprised. "Abraham, you sound as if Cats were created by *design*. Everybody knows they were a laboratory accident."

"No, no. I don't mean that at all! I only mean that when Cats were created, they did not come out as furry, four-footed human beings. They're so different from us physically that we forget how different they are from us mentally as well. The experiments which accidentally produced *Felis sapiens* created a whole new kind of animal, separate from the primates and distinct from other cats, too. Comparing Cats with humans is like comparing octopi with ants."

"Except that octopi are smarter than ants, I'm sure," said Hannah. "And no one knows if Cats are smarter than humans."

Hannah's father clapped his hands together and pointed at her. "That helps to support my argument, don't you see? We cannot even compare the two animals' intelligence properly because their brains function so differently that we are unable to use the same testing devices for both."

"That's all very well," said Hannah's mother. "But how do you explain the fact that some of our greatest artists and poets are Cats? Doesn't that count for creativity?"

Hannah's father squared his shoulders. "Music," he said with conviction, "is different. I do not know how. I do not know why. But humans will be the only masters of that art on Earth."

There was clearly no reply to this statement. "Time for tea," Hannah heard her mother say quietly as she rose to clear the table. It had been a typical dinner discussion at the Markuses, and also, typically, one that ended in a blind alley created by her father. The sheer normalness of it made Hannah feel warm and comfortable.

She went to bed early that night, to the sweet sounds of her father practicing his recital program.

Just as Abraham Markus had hoped, the recital was a happy success. Artist friends and other well-wishers clustered around Hannah's father afterward, bestowing kisses and hushed words of praise. The great Museum Hall emptied out slowly, as if the audience were lingering over the last fading notes.

As Hannah and her parents turned to go, two feline figures emerged from the aisle and moved toward them.

Agnes and Putney! thought Hannah. The excitement and agonies of the past week came flooding back over her.

The Cats greeted Hannah's father warmly and fell into step with the excited cluster of people. Hannah plodded behind the group, hurriedly trying to sort out her feelings.

Until the moment she saw Agnes and Putney, Hannah had been content to think only about what was happening around her. Suddenly she was burning with a need to be with them. She mustn't miss anything; she was a partner and she felt the separation acutely.

As if in answer to Hannah's thoughts, Putney fell behind the crowd and came alongside her.

"I must speak with you," he whispered.

"What's the matter?"

"Wait," he said. "Tell your parents you'll go back

with me. Then we can get on the ped belt after the others." He nudged her forward with his nose.

Hannah did as she was told. Her parents, exuberant from the success of the concert, agreed readily and went back to their conversations. Agnes was engrossed in a discussion with two rotund violinists and seemed unaware of either her brother or Hannah.

They let the crowd move on, gaining distance from them. Then Putney spoke.

"I'm worried about Agnes' state of mind. She seems awfully nervous," he said as they left the museum.

It was hard to imagine Agnes getting really nervous about anything. Angry or excited maybe, but not nervous. "Why?" Hannah asked.

"Well, last night, after you left, a very strange thing happened. I walked into Agnes' bedroom to call her for dinner and found her in the middle of a huge mess of papers. Margo Krupp's notes were scattered all over the room, and Agnes was picking them up. She asked me to help her get them back in order. When I questioned her about it, she just looked at me as if *I* had done something wrong."

"Was she trying to cover something up?"

"I don't know. I can't imagine what was going on in her mind or why she would have thrown those papers around. She's terribly orderly, normally."

"Yes, I know," said Hannah, remembering Agnes' desk with its neat piles and labeled drawers. "But what can *I* do about it?"

"Just help me keep an eye on her, will you? Obviously this project is bigger than any we have ever taken on. I'm frightened she may be feeling too much strain."

The party was underway by the time the two latecomers walked in. Hannah's father, now robed in a trailing gown of bright red, had set up an impromptu bar in the Pit and was eloquently offering marijuana, catnip, and mixed drinks to a half-dozen guests. Her mother, still in the long, dark, mesh tube dress she had worn to the concert, sat quietly on a cushion by the window with three or four other people. Cats and humans milled about as the strains of taped music floated through the air.

"I find Stokman *so* inspiring to listen to," one of the fat violinists remarked. He was standing near the doorway, looking down at Agnes, who was taking sniffs from a small cup of catnip before her. She caught sight of Hannah and winked at her.

"Oh, is that Stokman on the tape?" Agnes asked. "I thought it was Rachmaninoff."

The violinist smiled patronizingly. "Really, dear," he said, "there's nearly a century between the two composers. They are from entirely different schools!"

"A century? How silly of me," said Agnes and padded straight over to Hannah and Putney.

"What a bore!" she whispered to them. "I couldn't think of any other way to get loose from him than to appear stupid."

Putney shrugged. "What I need," he said, "is a large drink of water and a long sniff of catnip. Excuse me, females." He slipped away between the guests and leapt gracefully into the Pit.

As soon as he was gone, Agnes glanced around. "May I speak with you privately, Hannah?" she whispered.

What next? thought Hannah, but she nodded and led the way to her bedroom.

"Hannah, something terrible has happened," said Agnes when they had shut the door.

Hannah stood between her desk and the window, and looked at Agnes, wondering what to say. She could feel the agitation in the Cat's mind.

Agnes did not wait for a reply. She began pacing the narrow width of the room, talking rapidly. "About five o'clock Friday, I went out for some milk and left Putney to cook dinner. I was only gone about twenty minutes. When I got back, I put the milk on the counter and went to my room.

"I found it a shambles! At first I thought it was burglars, but then I realized Putney would have seen them come in. There's only one entrance to the apartment, of course. I didn't know what to think next. The notes were scattered all over the room; they were all mixed up."

Agnes jumped onto Hannah's bed and sat down on her haunches. "I don't care about the mess, really," she said. "The papers can be sorted. It's Putney's going in there and doing those things that's driving me crazy. And when he came into my room later, he acted as if he didn't know a thing about it."

Hannah stared at her friend. She was expecting a confession but had heard an accusation. Her thoughts whirled in circles. Either Putney or Agnes was lying to her, but she couldn't tell which of them was. She couldn't imagine either of them ever lying to her. And whoever was doing it was also acting bizarrely. Hannah began to get scared.

Agnes licked nervously at the sides of her mouth. "I don't know," she muttered. "Maybe Putney's jealous; he's not nearly as good at merging as I am. Maybe he thinks I'm better at it because I was Margo's friend."

"Do you think that was why he objected to our speeding up my learning sessions?" asked Hannah, knowing as she did that it couldn't be true. But what *was* true?

"The moon, the heavens, and the faraway stars know," sighed Agnes.

And then Hannah felt it—the chill of another presence, listening, waiting.

"Agnes," she said, "do you feel something? Somebody, here in the room?"

"What?" said Agnes. "Where?" She looked around her. "Yes, come to think of it, I do feel a . . . someone." Her eyes darted toward the window.

Hannah looked. Did the curtain waver? Did the light shift subtly outside her window, by the balcony? A burst of noise from the next room quickly drowned out other sensations. Hannah blinked and the chill melted away like dying snowflakes.

6

"Using molded parts was really a good idea for getting the shapes right," Hannah announced over the hubbub in the huge Number 2 Projects Room. "But I can see that balance is going to be a problem."

She and her partners were clustered around a table littered with hundreds of different-colored plastic triangles, trapezoids, rectangles, and squares—the unassembled product of their collective mind—the geometrics project.

Paul Ostrof stood beside Hannah, shaking his head. He sighed. "At least we didn't try to put this together till you got back."

"If she'd been here last week when we decided to make them out of molded plastic, she could have stopped us." It was Margaret Standish, no less drained of venom for Hannah's presence.

Hannah drew herself up angrily but Paul stepped in.

"Shut up," he fired point-blank at Margaret. "I want to hear about balancing." He turned to Hannah. "*I'm* glad you're back, anyway."

"Thanks, Paul." Hannah smiled at him, then caught a glimpse of Susan smirking in the background. She winked at Susan, then turned her attention back to the project.

"The reason it won't work," Hannah explained, "is that the model will be top-heavy. There won't be enough weight at the bottom to keep it from toppling over."

"How do *you* know?" Grace put in.

Hannah shrugged her shoulders. "I just do," she said. She wasn't sure how she knew either. It was a feeling she had, one that was new to her. She felt—acquainted with things that didn't move.

"I say we put it together and see what happens," said Margaret. "Then if it doesn't work, we'll figure out what to do next."

"I suppose that's reasonable," replied Hannah, watching the steam go out of Margaret's anger. "We can always add weights in the appropriate places afterwards, but the trick will be to figure out where to add them. That may be more difficult than any of the other parts of designing this model have been."

Paul, as project leader, called for a vote. "Those in favor of starting to assemble the model now, raise paw or hand."

Six limbs went up. The third Cat in the group, Jonathan, who never said much, joined in on the vote when he saw the others waiting for him.

"Well, it's decided unanimously," Paul said, putting his hand down. He made a notation in his lab book, then put it aside.

Painstakingly, the six partners began fitting the shapes together, sliding the grooved edges into each other—triangle to triangle, square to square, following the diagrams they had worked out during the previous months. As they put the pieces together, the different colors formed themselves into distinct designs within each separate substructure. Finally they had five three-dimensional shapes on the worktable. They began slowly fitting each shape to the next until a wobbling tower stood, held by three pairs of hands and three broad paws.

Susan gritted her teeth as she stretched to keep a grip on the upper edges of the model. "I *know* what's going to happen if we let go. An hour and a half of assembling and a week of parts construction down the drain."

The model teetered ominously. "We can't stand here forever," said Paul. "Let's try to take the substructures apart and talk this problem out." They carefully worked the five shapes apart and placed them back on the table. Everyone sat down, looking tired and discouraged.

Margaret spoke first. "OK. What's the idea now? If we don't think of something fast, we could miss the deadline altogether." She glared at Hannah as if it were all her fault.

Hannah glared back. "I don't have an idea yet," she answered. "Except to go to lunch."

Everyone looked up at the wall clock. It was nearly noon. There was no point in pushing things that day. They agreed to leave the model pieces as they were and meet the next morning with more energy and as many good ideas as they could find. Everyone took a few minutes to record the day's events in their lab books.

The room gradually emptied of noise and people. Susan stood over Hannah. "Come on. Let's go to lunch."

Hannah sat eyeing the pieces of the model. "You go ahead," she said to Susan. "I have some ideas after all."

"Look," said Susan. "You don't have to feel responsible for this, you know. No one's expecting you to work overtime because you missed school last week. Anyway, I thought you said you didn't have any ideas."

"I just got one. I want to try something in private." She waved Susan away. "I'll meet you in the dining hall."

Susan gave Hannah a long look. "All right," she said finally. "Suit yourself." She strode across the room and shut the door behind her.

Hannah stood up slowly, staring at the pieces of

the model. If she could just get a better feel for where to place the weights . . .

The figure nearest her was a blue-and-white rectangle, meant to form part of the base of the model. It seemed to rest comfortably enough on the table. Hannah reached forward and placed her left hand gently against its side. She closed her eyes and concentrated on losing her boundaries. Then slowly, she pressed her hand forward. The rectangle inched away in response to the pressure.

Hannah tried again. She thought hard: There are no boundaries—and slipped slowly away into her new consciousness. Her hand moved forward and melted into the rectangle, half in, half out. All was still for a minute.

Hannah searched with her mind, trying to sense the whole shape of the rectangle. She couldn't feel her palm or tell where it was. Instead, she began to sense the thin, flat shape of the entire rectangle— through her arm. She could feel its corners and its edges, the way it met with the surface of the table and rested there, perfectly balanced. Hannah could feel no tension in the way the rectangle stood. She withdrew her hand.

The rectangle *seemed* stable. But there was no point of comparison. What did an unstable shape feel like when you merged with it? The next thing was to try a structure that might have more problems in its construction, like the triangle.

Hannah put her hand to her face and felt sweat on

her forehead. Merging was hard work. But maybe, just maybe, she could find the weak points in the model this way and fix them faster and better than anyone else could. She wiped the sweat off on her coveralls and moved down the table to the triangle.

Her hand melted into the triangle with ease this time. No tension. Maybe the idea was wrong. Maybe you couldn't tell anything about balance and stress points by merging with an object.

Hannah withdrew her hand and moved on to the next shape on the table, a sphere. Her hand went in and—there! There was pressure, a lot of it, at the point where the sphere rested on the table. Hannah felt the weight of the sphere pressing down on that small spot and the stress radiating out from that point. It strained the equator of the sphere, and strained the upper half of the shape as well.

Slowly she slid her right hand under the sphere and raised it off the table. Immediately the pressures her left hand was feeling through the globe were released. The weight was being distributed over a larger area—her right palm—instead of a single plastic part about two square centimeters. She put the sphere down again and took her hand out of it.

"Well, I've learned one thing. You can feel stress when you merge. But I haven't solved the problem." The sphere was to rest in a circular hole in a rectangle. When it was in position, there would be very little stress of the kind Hannah had just felt.

She tried the last two shapes, just to be thorough,

but by then she had realized it was necessary to put the model together, at least partially, in order to find out how it balanced.

She felt exhausted. The rest of the testing would have to wait till another time.

It wasn't until she had left the classroom and was trudging toward the dining hall that it dawned on Hannah that she had actually merged, several times, completely on her own. A new wave of pride and excitement crowded out her fatigue. Glowing inwardly, she stepped into the dining hall.

Half of the school's one thousand students milled around in the enormous, low-ceilinged dining hall. The younger ones scurried around with lunch trays in their hands or, if they were Cats, with baskets in their mouths, and gathered in the left section of the hall, near the food line. The middle section was occupied by the oldest students, who sat in tight clusters on the floor in front of long, low tables, talking among themselves. Hannah's class and the two classes older than hers filled the section on the right. She moved to the tables at the back of the room by the window.

Paul and Susan were whispering to each other as Hannah knelt down beside them.

"Hi, folks! I'm back," she said cheerfully.

Abruptly the dialogue ended. Paul and Susan greeted Hannah and an uncomfortable silence ensued.

Hannah stood up again. "Well, I'm going to get lunch. Excuse me."

"Did you get the balance problem figured out?" Paul asked.

"No, but I'm working on it," said Hannah. "Maybe tomorrow."

"Gee, that's great. How did you do it?" Susan's voice was singsongy.

"What's for lunch?" asked Hannah, peering over their heads at their trays. "Bean pie?"

Susan's face turned stony. "Yeah, same thing we always have on Mondays."

The two girls' eyes met momentarily. Then Hannah looked away. "Be back in a minute," she said, and moved off toward the food line.

The line at the food counter was short by the time Hannah got to it. Margaret and Grace, the handles of their food baskets gripped between their teeth, and their tails held up high, were padding away to their own corner where they and their friends always ate.

A hateful bunch, thought Hannah, taking a tray of food. Always gossiping about someone, always sticking to each other as if no one else were worth associating with. She glanced down at her tray, where a small bowl of plain yogurt, a tiny cube of meat, and a bean pie sat patiently. Secretly, Hannah liked bean pie, and a lot of other ordinary foods, but such an attitude was unpopular at school. She tried to stay out of most discussions about school food because of this.

"Vegetable?" asked a fat, uniformed man behind the counter. Hannah made a quick scan of the list tacked up on a board behind the man. "Carrots and spinach, please," she told him. Two dishes were dropped efficiently onto her tray, and Hannah moved on. She chose banana milk from the shelves of drinks and decided against taking a piece of fruit.

On her way back, she had an impulse to avoid Paul and Susan and move to an empty table. She squelched it, knowing they would regard her all the more suspiciously if she did. She thought of their whispering and the look Susan had given her. It was plain that they had been talking about her. But what had she done? Was she acting strangely? Was her ability to merge somehow showing on her face? The idea of a confrontation was frightening. She couldn't tell them a thing about what had been going on. Why didn't they just go away?

Her wish came true, but not the way she wanted it to. Just as Hannah reached the table, Paul stood up.

"I've got to do some last-minute work on an essay," he muttered, gathering up his tray and backpack. "See you at dinner."

Hannah sat down. Susan turned her black eyes on Hannah and spoke in a hard voice.

"OK, Hannah. I can't take any more secrets. Something is happening to you, something big, and you're acting as if you don't trust me, like I'm not your friend or something. Tell me what is going on. Please."

Hannah knew her lip was trembling. "Nothing," she answered, feeling Susan's hurt like a stone hurled against her. "Nothing is going on."

Susan turned away. It was their last conversation for a long time.

⟨⟩ 7 ⟨⟩

The balance problem refused to get worked out. Hannah tried, after dinner and the next day before lunch, to assemble the substructures on her own. But she could never get the parts put together, hold on to them, and merge all at once. On Wednesday, she tried leaning the assembled parts against a cabinet so she wouldn't have to hold them up. But that threw the balance off in an unnatural way. The others in her project had no more luck than she. They all tried adding little lead weights to different places on the model, but inevitably it toppled.

Hannah thought about the problem a lot that week.

She avoided Susan as much as possible, concentrating on the project and on making up work in her afternoon writing class.

She met with Fern Samelson to discuss her progress. Her advisor seemed cool and businesslike.

On Thursday, she took her telepathy lesson and felt her instructor watching her with curiosity as she went through her exercises. There was an unspoken code that forbade ESP teachers to probe their students' minds for any reasons other than instruction. For once, Hannah was really glad of it.

There suddenly seemed to be too many observant, concerned people in her life. And somehow, the tables had gotten turned. School was no longer a secure, predictable refuge; it was a place where Hannah was being watched and criticized. When the weekend came, she left with a sense of relief.

That Saturday morning Hannah felt refreshed walking up Eastman Boulevard toward Agnes' apartment building. The morning sun shone brilliantly along the upper edges of towering, closely nestled buildings, though cool shade still enclosed the street itself. Hannah pulled her sweater collar up, enjoying warmer feelings of that morning's home-cooked breakfast and the lingering memory of her parents' brief good-bye hugs. She had gotten a bonus from them: permission to stay at the Brancusis until Sunday noon.

Agnes greeted Hannah at the door of her apartment. She was bright-eyed and her billowing black-

and-white fur looked lustrous. Even the long hair on her paws, which Agnes always said was a nuisance, looked soft and shiny.

"You're looking good this morning," Agnes said to Hannah, ushering her inside.

Hannah grinned and shrugged. She very nearly returned the compliment to Agnes, but couldn't muster the courage. That was the kind of thing grown-ups said.

Putney stepped out of the kitchen, a towel slung over his neck. "Hello, Hannah. How did your week go?"

Hannah swallowed the sudden lump in her throat. "Terrible," she said. "I'm not a good actress. Everybody knows I'm hiding something." She laughed nervously. "They're right, too."

"You just hang on," Agnes said. "Don't breathe a word of this to anyone."

"Don't worry," Hannah said. "Hey! I almost forgot! I did some merging all on my own this week."

"You *what?*" Agnes almost wailed. "Did anybody see you?"

Hannah walked past the Cats into the living room. "No, no, no one saw me. Listen, Agnes. I was using the merging to work on this geometrics project we're doing. I got into some plastic models to try to figure out how they balance and fit together."

"What do you mean 'got into'?" said Putney, tossing the towel aside. "You went all the way in? You don't even know how to do that."

"I just used my hand. No, not even that, only my palm. I haven't got the problems worked out yet, but I could *feel* where they are. It's really fantastic! I could actually feel the shape of the model, as if I were part of it."

"Yes, I can imagine," said Putney. He took a deep breath. "I'm not sure I approve of your merging alone. You could end up in trouble."

"He's right," said Agnes. "That was a dangerous thing you did. Even Putney and I don't merge without the other one nearby. It's so new to us that there's no way of even knowing what the real risks are."

Hannah shrugged her shoulders and looked down at her feet, feeling suddenly like a little child. "At least you can't accuse me of being reluctant anymore."

"All the more reason for making the first part of our session an all-talk, no-action one," said Agnes. "It will cool you off a little and make you remember why you're here."

"Aw, come on, Agnes. I don't need to be cooled off."

Agnes drew herself up, her chest fur spreading outward. "Merging must never be done capriciously, Hannah. We're like babies in a room full of plugs and sockets. Only luck and a respectful fear of merging are going to keep us from stepping out into a void and disappearing altogether. We don't know a damn thing about it. Margo Krupp's notes are little more than a bare-bones how-to manual."

Hannah did not reply.

"All right then," said Agnes. "We would like to spend most of the day telling you about problems we've had along the way and hammering out new questions with you. You know just enough about merging to understand most of this discussion. The rest you can ask us about."

Hannah looked up. "You're getting ahead of me! How can I help you with new questions till I've learned to merge?"

"You *have* learned," Putney replied, "though you're still very much a novice. Anyway, we thought while you do your practicing, you could also help us wherever you're able to with the research. Of course, we'll have to wait to deal with a lot of our questions about human reactions till later."

"OK, I guess," said Hannah. "Start talking and I'll see how much I can follow."

"Hannah," said Agnes, sitting down, "Would you please bring the stack of notebooks on the left side of my desk out here?"

Hannah obediently headed for the bedroom. It would have taken Agnes much longer, since she would have had to bring each notebook in, one at a time, between her teeth. Some Cats wouldn't even have bothered with paper and books, or used opposables for writing. Tape recorders and pocket-sized computerdictas were designed and packaged for their convenience. But Agnes liked to keep to the old ways.

Hannah carried the half-dozen gray cardboard-bound notebooks to the living room and sat down, depositing them in the middle of the floor. Putney pulled the top book off the stack. Holding the back cover stable with a rear foot, he opened the notebook and began leafing through it. "Ah! Here we are: the summary," he said, about halfway through. "I've kept a rather loose account of matters which really puzzle us. So far, I must say, we've made very little headway with them."

"We've been so wrapped up in just getting ourselves though walls in one piece," said Agnes, "that we haven't had much time to do anything else except raise questions."

"What kinds of questions?" asked Hannah.

In reply, Putney pressed his notebook flat and pushed it toward Hannah.

She read the neatly written page before her.

How Is Process Affected?

Merged Object:
    Size in relation to merger
    Density (i.e., solid, liquid, gas)
    Shape complexity
    Life

The notes on the next few pages included a number of lines under the heading "Merger," and some entitled "Time," "Distance," and "Frequency." Hannah turned back to the first page.

"These are ideas you want to try out? I'm not sure I understand what they all are."

Putney got up and stood next to Hannah. He pointed to the first line. " 'Merged Object.' That's the thing you merge with." Hannah nodded. She understood that much.

"Now, 'Size in relation to merger.' That relates to the problem of how much density an object can tolerate."

"You've already lost me," said Hannah, scratching her head. "What's this about tolerating?"

"Hannah," said Agnes. "A thing can't just keep getting denser and denser, filling up with extra molecules. Sooner or later, it's going to call a halt."

Hannah shook her head in confusion.

"Putney and I have already worked a little on that one," said Agnes. "Based on Margo Krupp's findings, we know that if a big person, such as a Cat, tries to merge with a little thing, such as a dinner bowl, the dinner bowl rejects the Cat at a certain point, once it reaches its density saturation level. It just sort of gets too full. What we need to find out is how full it gets when this happens. Margo left us a hypothetical formula, but we need to test it out thoroughly."

"Then," said Hannah, "I might not have been able to put more than my palm into those shapes at school."

"Possibly," said Putney. "We don't really know. Anyway, this set of problems relates to the next item." He pointed at the open notebook again. "Presumably, liquids have more room for extra molecules than solids. And gases have more than liquids or solids."

"Merging into liquids?" said Hannah. That was difficult to imagine. But then, after all, it might be possible. Once you believed in merging, it wasn't really all that hard to extend its possibilities in your imagination. Instead of splashing around in a swimming pool, you could merge with the water in it. Hannah pictured herself disappearing as she slowly slipped into the water. Yes, maybe such a thing *could* happen.

She turned back to the notebook. "OK. What's next?" she asked Putney.

"Shapes," said Putney, "are defined quite differently in merging terms than by other terms. We must learn more about how merging can occur with multimaterial objects—things made of both metal and stone, for example. Also, things with complex contours—a long, curving sidewalk or an apartment building."

Hannah sat up straight. "Now I'm beginning to see why you've got so much work to do. Didn't Doctor Krupp get to any of this?"

"Oh, yes, some of it," Agnes answered. "But she worked alone, apparently. Her findings must be corroborated by extensive research. We'll do as much of that here as we can."

" 'Life.' What is 'life'?" Hannah was back to Agnes' outline.

Agnes looked at Hannah. "Ever thought about merging into another person? Do you think it could work? We're rather too scared to try it just now. And, since she worked alone, Doctor Krupp can't tell us much about it."

Hannah stared at Agnes in amazement. She barely had time for this new possibility to sink in before Agnes sat up sharply, her eyes darting around.

"I smell smoke!" she cried. Simultaneously, the two Cats turned toward the bedroom door; they had picked up the scent before Hannah did.

As Hannah looked over, a wisp of dusty white smoke trailed out from under the bedroom door. All three of them raced to the door and Hannah flung it open.

In the middle of an ancient rug, a pile of papers was smoldering. Little flames struck out into the air. Hannah grabbed a sleeping mat and flapped it down on the burning pile. Again and again she beat at the fire until, at last, it was only a heap of charred, ruined papers.

They stared at the pile for a moment. Then Putney stepped to the window to let out the smoke. "Look," he said. "A note." He pulled a torn bit of paper from the handle of the window and read: " 'You must cease this work. Go back to your other concerns before you too are caught in the web.' "

Agnes joined Putney. She read the message again, then peered down into the black mass on the floor. "It was the notes. All of Margo's notes," she said quietly.

Hannah looked up. "But who did it?" she asked, feeling a tightening knot of fear and anger in her throat.

Agnes shook her head and uttered two impossible words: "Margo Krupp."

8

"It can't be!" Hannah shouted.

"Are you mad?" asked Putney. "Margo Krupp is dead!"

"I know it can't be," said Agnes. "But it must be. No one else *could* have done it."

"What are you saying?" said Putney. "That a ghost has been here? Agnes, make some sense."

Agnes looked down at the ruin of notes. "It was either a ghost or a person who could function like a ghost—by *walking through walls*." She gestured toward the message. "Besides, this is Margo's handwriting."

There was a silence in the room.

"Of course," said Putney finally. "Who else could it possibly have been? The window was locked from the inside. But how could she be alive?"

"The heavens only know," said Agnes, running her paw across her face.

Putney's eyes darted to Agnes. "Then it *was* someone else who raided your desk last week."

Agnes nodded.

"I thought it was *you*," said Putney. "You must have thought it was *me*."

Agnes nodded again. "Margo may have been checking to be sure we had all the notes. I must have come back before she could destroy them that day."

"If she didn't want us to have them, why didn't she just take them?" asked Hannah.

Agnes shook her head. "She couldn't take them even if she wanted to. Paper can't merge, only people."

"So," said Putney, "Margo Krupp has come back to haunt us. But why hasn't she shown her face? How could she destroy her work? Why does she want us to stop?"

"Maybe ghosts don't show their faces," Hannah suggested.

"She's not a ghost," said Putney. "There are no ghosts. She *must* be alive. How she survived being lost in space or how she ever got back here is the real puzzle."

"Perhaps there was a botch-up in the report of her death."

74

"Perhaps," said Putney. "Perhaps."

Hannah pushed at the pile with the toe of her shoe. "Do you want me to try to clean this up?"

Agnes seemed to snap out of a dream. "Oh! Yes," she said. "The vacuum hose is in the wall beside the window. Get the worst of this mess up, and we'll worry about the rest later on. Don't touch anything that might be salvaged, though." She walked to the door, lost in thought. "Why? Why any of it?" she muttered. "Hurry up and clean, Hannah. We need to have a long talk."

The Cats left the room. Hannah heard the teapot being clunked onto the stove. She picked her way through the mess, stopping to gather up the larger charred pieces.

The upshot of it all was that they decided to do nothing about Margo Krupp—for the moment. They did not know how to find her, or what had made her do what she did.

"There seems to be no logic to her actions," Putney remarked as they sat in the living room once again.

"And that isn't like her," said Agnes. "She must not be the Margo I used to know. I admit there was an odd streak in her—a sort of driven aspect to the way she used to go at her work. But lots of dedicated people are like that. I didn't see much of her during the last couple of years. No one did, for that matter. She could have changed a great deal during that time."

A thought, something about school, flashed through Hannah's mind then, and flickered out.

"Maybe . . . maybe she changed just from doing her work," she said very quietly.

"Well," Agnes continued, "she's gotten rid of her notes. And she's made it clear what she wants *us* to do. But why didn't she just come to me directly?"

"And why is she keeping her very existence a secret?" asked Putney.

Agnes stood up and stretched. "There's nothing we can do," she said, sitting down again. "We're going to have to pick up where we left off and somehow muddle through without the help of the notes. It won't be easy either. It's a terrible blow to our work, not to mention the fact that those notes are irreplaceable. Hannah, why are you looking at me that way?"

"I . . . Agnes, oh!" Tears welled up in Hannah's eyes, but she bit her lip and held them back. "Agnes, is she going to do something to us? Is she going to hurt us?"

Putney put his paw over her hand. "She won't touch you," he said softly. "Each of us will look after the others."

She couldn't fight the tears. They came fast now, warming the chill of her fear, but not lessening its bite.

"Hannah," Agnes said, "none of us is hurt and no one will be, either."

"Why is she scaring us? We're not hurting *her*."

"Perhaps we are," Agnes replied, "in a way that we don't understand."

Putney stroked Hannah's hair. "We must tread softly now," he said.

The three seekers returned to their work. About Margo Krupp, there was nothing more to do or say. The Cats sat down with paper and pencil to reconstruct what they could remember of her notes. After two hours, they were strained from the effort.

"This is an enormous job," said Agnes. "But we must do it slowly. There's bound to be substantial loss, so let's be careful and try not to be hasty."

Putney agreed. They took a tea break and went on to other work.

The activity of the day turned to Hannah and moving her along on merging. Slowly her fears subsided as it became clear that Margo Krupp would not return, at least for some time. Hannah felt no fourth presence in Agnes' apartment. There were only the two Cats, guiding, protecting, coaxing her.

Now that she had merged a small portion of her body several times, Hannah found it fairly easy to progress—with a few exceptions.

It was the next time she moved her arm forward into the practice wall that she met with resistance, in the form of her watch. It simply wouldn't go in. It pressed against the wall and it strained against her arm, too, resisting Hannah's efforts to coax it in along with her. Agnes noticed her plight.

"Oh! Remember what I told you about paper not going through walls?" she said apologetically. "You can merge nothing but your own body."

Hannah looked at Agnes, first with irritation, then surprise, as she realized the full implications of what she was being told.

"It means no clothing, glasses, or artificial body parts. We just didn't think—since we hardly ever wear any clothing." Putney looked askance at Hannah. "You don't have any artificial parts, do you?"

"For pete's sake!" said Hannah, withdrawing her hand from the wall. "You're just lucky I don't. I could have gotten into that wall and left my heart or my liver lying on the floor. Wouldn't that have been nice?"

"Well, I doubt that it would have happened quite so dramatically," Agnes replied. "You might have felt some pressure against those organs, and then, so much resistance from your body that you could not have proceeded."

Hannah released most of her anger in a huff of breath. "Merging isn't for everyone, is it?"

The Cats shook their heads.

"I suppose I've got to strip now."

They nodded.

Cats certainly had no funny feelings about nakedness—they were always naked. Therefore, Hannah reasoned to herself, she should feel no embarrassment whatsoever over her own nakedness before them. Cats were used to a lack of clothing. What did they care if she took her clothes off? Resolutely she put her hand to the zipper on her coveralls.

The Cats just stood there waiting, looking blankly at her. It's a good cause, thought Hannah. Quickly she unzipped her coveralls and shed them along with shoes, socks, and underwear. Her watch and earrings went into the pocket of the coveralls. Hannah tried pretending she was a Cat. It would have been convenient to have fur right then.

"Just one more thing," said Agnes as Hannah stood, trying to find a place to put her arms. "Have you any fillings or false teeth?"

Hannah shook her head. She knew almost no one who had fillings or false teeth. Still, it was a good question to ask.

For a while after that, the merging went quite smoothly. Concentrating on the job at hand helped Hannah forget about her nakedness. She realized she had been right about the Cats, too. They didn't seem to be the least bit bothered.

When she was able to put one arm and shoulder into the wall, the Cats stopped her.

"You're going to have to head straight in, at this point," Agnes told her. "But there are some things you should know first."

Hannah sat down.

"How do you think you'll feel about putting your head into the wall?" Agnes asked her.

Hannah hadn't thought about that before. "That means I stop breathing. Like going underwater, I suppose."

"That's right," said Agnes, "but it isn't exactly like going underwater. When you're swimming," she explained, "you hold your breath because your body can't breathe water, and because you need the air that's in your lungs. When you merge, you don't hold your breath because you don't need the air."

"That doesn't make sense to me," said Hannah.

"Well, we don't wholly understand it ourselves," said Putney. "We know, though, that somehow the merger's body stops functioning except on a limited basis—it must be a form of suspended animation. We don't know just how this affects the body."

"Anyway," Agnes continued, "the point is not to worry about needing air. It's important to remember that because, as you know, any fear on your part may trigger your expulsion from the wall."

"I know," said Hannah, already feeling nervous.

"All right then. Now Hannah, please don't worry about failing. You can just keep trying until you get it right. OK?"

Hannah shrugged. "I'll try," she said.

Agnes padded over and stood between the wall and Hannah. "The other thing you must know is how to move within the wall and how to emerge from it. Before, you always had leverage. There was enough of you *out* to pull with physically."

"Now I won't have anything to pull with!"

"But do you realize that you were also pulling with your mind before?" Agnes asked.

Hannah thought. "Yes, I guess I was. Only I didn't really know I was then."

"You've been practicing for a complete merging all along," Agnes told her. "Just keep thinking *out* when you're ready to emerge. It'll happen."

"Where will I end up, though?"

"That's a guess, for now. You will learn to direct yourself pretty gradually." Agnes got up. "I think we'd better move the furniture away from this wall, though, just to make sure you don't wind up on top of my desk if you emerge in the bedroom. If it will help you at all, one of us can merge with the wall first—just to show you how it looks."

Hannah nodded, a little relieved. "I've never seen it," she said. "I've only watched you come out."

Moving the furniture took only a minute. Hannah thought about what it would be like to be stuck inside the wall, unable to send herself out of it. Putney must have been reading her feelings. He approached Hannah and told her, "We'll be right near, right next to the wall in case anything happens. We can even help pull you out if you start having trouble."

"Right, then," said Agnes, clapping her paws together, which made a sound like soft dough being spanked. She slipped a thin, gold necklace off her neck. Then she turned to face the wall, and instantly her back straightened with concentration. Slowly, gracefully, Agnes raised one fluffy paw and sent it into the wall. The rest of her followed in one easy Cat-motion: Her head disappeared next, then front legs and shoulders, chest and belly, haunches and rear legs—until the unruly white tip of her tail was all that remained. Then it flicked and was gone. No more Agnes.

Hannah had just enough time to release her breath before Agnes glided smoothly out again, facing forward. She came out walking, not falling this time, and looked as if she had just come back from an afternoon stroll. She sat down and cocked her head. "I'm getting much better at this," she said and closed her eyes in a proud, contented smile.

"That was beautiful," whispered Hannah.

Putney looked at her. "It was, wasn't it? Now it's your turn to be beautiful."

"Hah!" said Hannah, grinning. But inside she felt her nervousness growing.

She approached the wall tentatively. There was no putting it off anymore.

"Just do it the way you've been practicing it all along," said Putney, who had followed her there. "Move straight ahead and concentrate on becoming one with that wall. Trust it," he whispered coaxingly.

"Trust it," Hannah chimed and drew herself up flush with the wall. She placed her palms against it and closed her eyes. As soon as she felt her hands merging, Hannah stepped forward. She was surprised to feel herself gliding in smoothly and gracefully. Such a small, quiet step.

And then, Hannah was mind. All mind. There was suddenly no more than that. And it was wonderful, indescribable! She no longer had a body, but instead of feeling fear or loss, as the Cats had said she might, she felt tremendous gain.

"I'm free!" she shouted wildly in her mind. "No more arms and legs, no more breathing. No more gravity! Just me."

There was no physical sensation at all—at least

none Hannah had ever felt before. Her mind seemed to be floating loosely in a weightless void, yet she could sense the massiveness of the wall of which she was a part. She could not have said what she felt of that shape or how she felt it. She only knew that she understood its contours and its—wallness. But it didn't seem to restrict her; it held her mind the way it held the millions and billions of particles of her body: loosely, freely, yet carefully.

She hung in the great stillness of these feelings for some unknown length of time. Then, slowly, some sense of perspective returned. It was hard to grasp at first, but Hannah remembered that far, far away, Agnes and Putney were waiting for her and that she must think about leaving.

Though it was new to her, Hannah had no trouble dealing with the idea of directing herself out of the wall. She suddenly felt as if there were nothing she couldn't do. Quickly she drew up the image of Agnes' living room and the spot she had last stood on there. Out. I want out, she thought and concentrated hard on that wish.

She began to feel a strange shrinking sensation— the pulling together of her diffuse parts—and at the same time, she lost the feeling of the shape of the wall. Somehow there was a driving, a pressing toward one place. Then, a feeling of being sucked through an enormous drainpipe. And then, shock, as she plunged into the ice-cube bath of having a real body with all its ponderous deliberateness—and found herself sprawled on the floor with two Cats peering concernedly down at her.

Hannah shifted her limbs about and finally sat up, brushing her tousled hair away from her face. She felt dazed and wanted to just sit there and think about what had happened. Her body felt heavy—she had never known it to be like this before. Moving it seemed to require a great effort.

"How do you feel?" asked Agnes.

"Tired, I guess," said Hannah. "You never . . ."

"Do you know that you did that remarkably well, Hannah? As if you'd been doing it for ages! You even came out at the same spot you entered. It looked very smooth from here."

"How long was I in there?"

"Several minutes," replied Putney. "We were starting to worry. But then you came out, quite fast and all in one continuous movement. It was impressive, really."

"Minutes!" Hannah covered her face with her hands and tried to think clearly. There was so much to put into order. So much that didn't seem to fit into any of the usual compartments in her mind. "Why didn't you tell me about that feeling?" she asked the Cats, still hiding behind her hands. "About not having a body and feeling so wonderful and free and everything?"

There was no reply. Hannah lowered her hands and saw the Cats watching her with curiosity.

"What feeling?" asked Agnes.

"You know," Hannah urged. "All that power and space and . . ." The Cats stood there, incomprehension written on their faces.

Hannah put her hands in her lap. "You don't know," she said quietly. "You really don't know what I'm talking about, do you?" She looked from one Cat to the other as more realizations slowly came to her. "What *do* you feel?" she asked them.

Agnes' tail flicked to the side in a shrugging gesture. "We merge. We feel nothing, a void all around us. We think about getting out, and we leave. The question is, what do *you* feel?"

So Hannah began sorting out the incredible experience as she spoke, stopping along the way, going back and rephrasing, trying to make them understand something that couldn't be told. When she was finished, she knew, at least, that *they* knew there was nothing else like it. And that Hannah was the only one in that room who could ever really know what had happened to her.

They had all done the same thing. Yet Hannah's perception of it was a thousandfold heightened and utterly different from the Cats'.

"It must be because you're human," said Putney, shaking his head in amazement.

"Didn't Margo Krupp's notes say anything about it?" asked Hannah, feeling suddenly alone.

"Nothing," said Agnes. "If she felt the way you do about merging, she didn't record it in her notes."

That feeling, whatever it was, whatever its name

could be, made merging so much more than a mere process. It would have been hard to write about merging and leave that part of it out of the telling. Yet, Hannah felt sure, somehow, that Dr. Krupp *had* been through the same thing—that it was not she, Hannah, who was special, but humans in general and the way their minds worked.

There was something special about humans or something missing in Cats. Something that made Cats and humans very, very different from each other.

"I'm hungry," said Hannah, getting hurriedly to her feet. "And thirsty. Is it time for dinner yet?"

Agnes laughed a high, piercing-thin Cat-laugh. "Kids! They conquer mountains and think about food."

9

The three of them threw themselves into the tasks at hand: to learn the mysteries of merging—when, how, and where it worked—and to reconstruct the burned notes. They began chipping away at the mass of unanswered questions, making notes and setting up the experiments for solving the problems.

First came the question of the size of the object into which one merged. They made lists of different-sized objects to try out: a spoon, a table, a door. A stove, a desk, and so on. Hannah began making up a chart on each object for recording their results.

"We'll have to have each of us test each object, won't we?" she asked the Cats. "That way there'll be three different sizes of mergers: three different amounts of merging molecules to try."

"Good thinking," Putney replied. "Of course, we can't really be precise or come up with a formula until we can get exact density and weight measurements on us *and* the objects. But we're making some kind of start, at least."

They set up the solid-liquid-gas problem on charts, too. But obviously these experiments would have to wait until they could gain access to a properly equipped laboratory. Agnes and Putney each had a laboratory in the government ESP complex, but "A million eyes will be upon us there," as Agnes put it, "not to mention the fact that we'd need to order in mounds of suspicion-arousing materials, such as water tanks and airtight chambers for testing gases." Agnes flicked her ears in irritation. "There is something awfully sloppy about this work," she muttered, "but there's no way around it until we can answer the one question that lies behind all the others."

Putney, like a king pronouncing judgment, slowly closed his eyes and opened them in assent.

"What do you mean?" asked Hannah, not for the first time feeling left out. "What one question?"

"Why, the question of what we should do with this discovery," said Agnes. "Or rather, what human and Cat should do with it, if anything. Whether we are going to use it or abuse it—whether it's going to mean that walls are to become merely things that keep the weather out instead of insuring people's privacy. Whether the three of us are going to tell anyone about it at all."

"Don't be silly," said Hannah. "I don't understand why we can't just turn this discovery over to the proper authorities and let them go through all the experimentation. Or at least move to one of your laboratories."

"Hannah!" said Agnes, her eyes growing round. "The government is not entitled to this information— only I am, as a recipient of Margo Krupp's estate. That means that I, not the government, am to decide its fate."

Hannah stood up. "You can't do that! It's like inventing the wheel and then not telling anybody about it."

Agnes rose and planted her four feet firmly in place. She stood looking up at Hannah. "I can and I will be the one to decide," she said. "There is no universal law about sharing knowledge, as far as I know. Now, let's get on with the plans." She moved back to the pile of notes and charts on the floor.

But wasn't there a universal law? thought Hannah. An unspoken one, yes, but a law just the same? Could Agnes really be intending to suppress the knowledge of merging? Horrified, Hannah suddenly realized what Agnes' decision could mean for her. She had been trusted not to tell *now*; she might be asked not to tell forever.

She turned away from the Cats, toward the window. An accomplice, that was what she was. Some kind of underground schemer, hiding a precious gift of knowledge.

She set her jaw. She had that knowledge, too. And Agnes couldn't stop her from giving it to other people. If Agnes decided not to tell, then she, Hannah, would. There would be no . . .

"Come on, Hannah." Putney was at her side, a paw curled around her wrist. "We'll deal with all that later. We need you now. Come back."

She moved to join Agnes, who was again scribbling notes on a writing tablet. But Hannah's mind was not on the next experiment.

⊛10⊛

"Really, you won't believe it. You'd have to have been there to appreciate it. It was another big blunder for the bumbling Buffoon."

Marla, a big, darkly marked Cat who roomed with Hannah, was talking about the school's favorite object of laughter—a teacher whom students long ago dubbed the Buffoon. All ten roommates of room 7 were sitting around on the floor that evening, or leaning out of their sleeping cells, enjoying a rare pre-bedtime moment together.

Titters and a cry of "Let's have it!" were heard

around the room, and Marla settled in to her story, curling a fat brown tail around her paws.

"Well, we were having supercatch practice in the big gym on sublevel 3. But today Coach Oakley couldn't make it—a sore paw or something. Anyway, the season's officially over, so we were planning a loose session with a game, but no drills or anything like that.

"We got there and we couldn't believe our eyes— the Buffoon was subbing for Coach. I mean, what could she possibly tell us that we didn't already know?"

"What *did* she tell you?" asked Susan. They all knew the Buffoon couldn't resist a chance to give advice.

Marla laughed. "She *showed* us! She actually showed us. We're right in the middle of a play and Farley from level 20 sends a long pass down to me. I had my mouth open, all ready to catch the ball. I took a leap into the air but the Buffoon stepped in front of me.

" 'Position!' she shouts and catches the ball. She stuffs it into her mouth—no, really! Stuffs it into her mouth like she's a Cat, and makes a run for it. She got tackled in about two seconds, needless to say. Except that it took two of us to get her down because she's so much bigger than we are."

"Incredible," said Gerta, another Cat. "Did you ever find out why she did it?"

Marla stood up and shrugged her shoulders

slightly. "I think she was trying to show us how easy it would have been to intercept that pass by an opponent. But I was way ahead of her on that score. I'd already checked the field—there wasn't another opponent nearby to intercept. Except the Buffoon."

Everyone roared their appreciation. Then Susan got up. "Anyone for a nightcap?" she said. "I'm going down to the canteen and I can bring something up."

By the time orders were taken, it was clear another pair of hands was needed. Susan looked at Hannah, who had been sitting on the other side of the room. "Come on," she said.

Hannah got to her feet. It seemed to require a great effort just to stand up. She'd been feeling tired ever since Monday, when the school grind had begun again. Hannah threaded her way toward the door through an obstacle course of seated and prone figures.

"How's the studying going for you?" Susan asked as soon as they were in the hallway.

Hannah stared ahead of her as she walked, trying to puzzle out the tone in Susan's voice. This was the first time in three years she had been practically on her own for final week preparations. She and Susan had gone their separate ways ever since that time in the dining hall, speaking to each other only when their work on the project required it.

"It's going OK," she answered. "I'm still not happy about the geometrics model, though."

"We've got the problem almost solved," said Susan.

Her voice seemed to register no hint of the recent tension between them. "The weights are nearly all in place. We just have to pull our notes together for a report."

"Well, the report's usually the hardest part, as far as I'm concerned. And we never did figure out a real system for attaching the weights. All we ever did was fiddle with them until they worked. That will go down badly with the Grading Committee."

"You're a perfectionist, Hannah," said Susan. "I know it's nice to know how and why everything works, but sometimes it's all you can do just to get it to work."

They had reached the elevator. Hannah punched the button with force. "If only there were more time!" she muttered. "I could get those weights in with some kind of precision, instead of the way we just slide them around till they do what we want them to do."

Susan looked hard into Hannah's eyes. "But could you tell the committee how you did it?"

Hannah backed away and the words hung in the air between them.

"What?" she whispered, panic tightening on her throat like a hand.

Susan unrelentingly repeated her question. "Could you tell the committee how you did it? Could you even tell me?"

Hannah swallowed and tried to think of an answer. She found none. Only questions that sprung up like tautly pulled wires. Was Susan her friend? What did

Susan know? What could Hannah possibly tell her to get her off the track?

"No," she said at last, feeling trapped. "I couldn't tell anyone."

Susan nodded. "I thought so," she said. "And I know what you're thinking. You're wondering how much I know about you." The elevator arrived and the two of them stepped into it.

Susan held up one hand and marked off each finger as she spoke. "You have a secret that gives you some special kind of . . . ability to see things people don't usually see or do things not ever done, or something like that. You learned about it away from school and you're still involved in it. And now you're scared. Have I got it right so far?"

Hannah nodded, not believing her ears. "How did you know?"

"Hannah," Susan answered, "you radiate secretiveness. You make excuses to me and then sneak off to perform experiments on the geometrics model. You come back acting like you've been to Mars or something.

"You weren't really honest with me. You told me you weren't in trouble. How can I keep all this to myself if I know that?"

"I'm not in trouble, Susan." The words pushed out through Hannah's mouth.

Susan turned a cold glance toward Hannah. "*I* think you are. And I think you owe it to me to be straight about it."

Hannah stared hard at the floor. In the silence that

filled the elevator, her thoughts came like bullets, hot and fast. Susan was going to tell. She was going to make Hannah tell her all the rest and then she was going to tell somebody else. Hannah recoiled from the horror of this trap and suddenly wanted only to get away, to disappear until Susan had forgotten about her.

She stepped back and felt the sheltering right-angle walls of the elevator. It came to a stop, the door opened, and Susan stepped forward into the hallway.

"Come on," she said and turned to face Hannah. Hannah rushed out ahead of Susan and disappeared down a side hallway. By the time Susan had looked up and down the corridors in that section of the building, Hannah was nowhere to be seen.

Returning to the elevator, Susan picked up the heap of Hannah's clothing that was lying there and stared at it in disbelief for a moment. Then she hurried away.

In minutes, a security squad was pacing the halls, knocking on doors, inquiring, and checking darkened laboratories, elevator shafts, and gyms. Susan had gone back to room 7 and she and her roommates were already spreading out through the halls of level 22, looking for Hannah.

Hannah drifted, unknown dimensions away. She rode the elevator shaft, hummed with the elevator's motor, and felt its great weight climb and dip, climb and dip.

Once, the door opened and a girl and a Cat got on.

She could feel their extra weight and the pressure of their feet against the floor. If she could have seen then, she would have watched the hackles on the Cat's back rise, his tail fanning, the confused look in his eyes as he wondered why he suddenly felt fear. The elevator stopped, and the girl and the Cat left, speaking in low tones and hurrying down the corridor.

When Hannah emerged from the elevator, it was stationary, its door opened at the top of its climb, the floor where Hannah's room was. Without hesitating, she hurried down the hallway and slipped into the stairwell that led to the roof.

It was a deep, clear night and the sky's bowl circled Hannah and held her from a billion miles away. Hannah hugged herself, for comfort more than for warmth, and sat down. She leaned back against the wall of the stairwell and watched the stars. They seemed to be filled with their own calm. She did not remember closing her eyes.

"Hannah Markus?" The clipped feline voice jolted her awake. Hannah opened her eyes and gazed fuzzily into the face of the security patrol Cat.

"You'll have to come with me now," he said. Hannah got up slowly and obediently fell into step behind the Cat. She wondered where they were going, but did not think of running. She felt very tired.

Hannah's roommates were back in room 7 by the time she and the patrol Cat got there. Their talking ceased as one by one they turned to watch her get

dressed. Susan stood at the front of the group, un-
moving. Then Hannah and the Cat left for the elevator.

As soon as the Cat pushed the button marked *12,*
Hannah knew what she would be facing. It would be
worse than the security patrol. Worse than Susan.

Behind the long glass wall, a single light shone. It
lit up the small, yellow office and the seated figure
behind the desk. The patrol Cat left Hannah at the
door.

Fern Samelson looked up as Hannah came in. "Do
you want to tell me about this?" she asked.

Anger rose up inside Hannah. "Susan ratted on
me, didn't she? She had to report me. She couldn't
just let me be, could she?"

Fern Samelson cocked her head to one side. "What
does Susan have to do with this?"

"She told Security I disappeared, didn't she?"

"Wouldn't you have done the same?"

"I . . ." Hannah closed her eyes against the tears
that fought their way up so quickly. She took a long,
ragged breath and then, resigned, asked, "What did
she tell you?"

"Nothing," her advisor replied.

"Nothing?"

"I have not spoken with Susan," said Fern. "Security told me that Susan had reported you missing.
They phoned my quarters as soon as they found you.
I want to speak with you, Hannah. I want you to talk
to me."

Hannah sat down and let the tears out. Quietly she

cried, her eyes closed against Fern's gaze. Then, after long minutes, she took the handkerchief Fern had placed at the edge of the desk.

"There isn't anybody I can tell," Hannah said softly. "I want to, but I can't. Not now. Maybe soon, but not now."

Fern Samelson's voice was quiet, with gentle urging behind it. "Perhaps there is just one person you could tell, who wouldn't tell another living soul."

"I promised the Brancusis! I promised myself, at least until I could find out whether they would decide to suppress this. If they do, then I'll have to tell it myself. But not now. Not yet." She clenched her jaw and the tears started again.

"Hannah, you're having a terrible time! I have watched you and I know you're not happy. Whatever the Brancusis have told you to do, it is a tremendous burden." She slammed her front paws down hard on the desk. "Why must a child be given such a job?"

"That doesn't matter!" Hannah blurted out. "What we're doing is more important than what's happening to me. Besides, the Brancusis say it's too dangerous to tell about—till we know more, and maybe not even then. . . ."

Fern Samelson came over to Hannah and looked closely into her face. "Hannah, it's *you* that matters now. The Brancusis care about their work. But I care about you. It's time you thought about yourself a little. And about the things that used to matter to you a few weeks ago."

And so, hearing her own voice with surprise, Hannah began. The Cat sat near her in silence, her eyes growing round with amazement, then narrowing with intense consideration. Hannah talked until her voice grew weary. She talked until the night-lights blinked on in dimmed corridors, the lights of sleeping quarters went out, and quiet filled every other corner of Whole School. And then, finally, she was through.

"I will not step into your private world," said Fern Samelson after Hannah was done. "If I did that, it would mean a break in a seal of trust, and probably the end of your experiments. I do not know if the Brancusis are right. But I agree with you about keeping the secret for now."

"Fern Samelson?" said Hannah.

"Yes?"

"I feel better now. Just telling you, you know. And I really want to keep working with Agnes and Putney."

Her advisor nodded. "There is little else I can offer you right now, other than to listen to you. But you can come to me anytime you want. And no one else will hear about this from me."

"Thank you," said Hannah.

"I hope you'll be able to deal with your life better than you have been recently."

Hannah shrugged. "I'll try not to run anymore, if that's what you mean. But Susan . . ."

Fern Samelson smiled with her eyes. "I'll take care of Susan, without satisfying her curiosity. I think if she feels I have you 'under wraps,' she'll be less inclined to meddle. I hope you two can be friends again after this is over."

Hannah stood up. She was wearier than she could ever remember having been before.

"Try to be strong," said Fern Samelson. "Try to hold on to the old Hannah who knows so well how to do things and how to be happy."

"Fern Samelson? Do I have to be grown-up all of a sudden? Do I have to do everything perfectly?"

Fern Samelson laughed. "No. But sometimes people do have to grow in big leaps instead of little, careful steps." She reached out her paws, and Hannah held her hand forward to be taken, as the two of them had done in that same room, one big leap ago.

11

In a way, thought Hannah, as she emerged from the monorail station at Bissell Street, it had been easier not to have gone into the city last weekend, not to have worked with Agnes and Putney. Like many others, she had stayed at school to study for her finals. Hannah had found the peace and the hours to dig into her work, with little time for thought as to what was happening outside.

Though results would not be sent home for two weeks, she knew she had done well in her courses. She had made up for lost time. The geometrics project had been dealt with in the best way, the proper way—imperfectly, but without further complications.

Her roommates and friends had left her alone. But it was far better than being hounded. Besides, Hannah needed that time all to herself.

And then, exams over, she had packed her bag in that familiar room in which she had lived and to which she would return the following fall. Back home, she had found a bright orange scarf stuffed into a side pocket of her suitcase, with a note from Susan wishing her a good summer. She had lifted the scarf up and it had trailed, flowing to the floor.

Now it was back to another kind of work—the work of merging. But going back was easier now. Hannah felt as if a great weight had been lifted from her shoulders and heart. School was finished, and finished well. The complicated ties of that world were severed for the summer.

Now that it seemed farther away, Hannah wondered how she could have handled things differently. More gracefully, for one, she thought, remembering the excuse she'd made to get away from Susan so she could work alone in the projects room. She might have tried caring more about Susan and her other friends, too. Caring about how they might have felt when she left them for her private world of merging. But no, she couldn't have cared more. There had been too much to worry about as it was.

And too much to fear, as well, like being found

out. She'd merged practically in front of Susan's nose—a terrible risk in a moment of panic. But what else could she have done? Probably Agnes or Putney would have known, but not she, not Hannah the Kid Scientist. Once more, she felt inadequate to handle the situation. She knew it wouldn't be the last time either.

And through all of these thoughts, there flowed a strange current of excitement that had been with Hannah ever since her last visit to Agnes' apartment. It was the memory of total merging, that sense of freedom and of power that came from being released from her body. Hannah held this deep and secret feeling close inside her, and let herself dream for a moment of having it again in full force.

"How is our colleague and ace student?" Agnes' voice sang out from the bedroom as Putney opened the front door for Hannah. Hannah returned Putney's smile and called out, "Glad to be back."

"I'll be right there," said Agnes. Hannah turned to Putney.

"What's new on this front?"

Putney shrugged. "A little and a lot," he said. "I've been back to my lab, and so has Agnes. We have to show our faces there from time to time, just to prove we still exist."

"It must be nice not having to answer to anybody," said Hannah.

Putney laughed. "Oh, we answer, all right! You

should see the reports and papers we have to produce when our grants come up for renewal. True, no one watches us on a day-to-day basis, but work must be done anyway. You at least have the summer off."

"Not really," Hannah said. "I'm starting piano lessons on Monday." She sat down on the living-room floor. "What do you plan to write about merging for all your reports and papers?"

"Everything," said Putney, "or nothing. We will cross that bridge when we come to it."

There was the big question again: whether merging was to be a temporary secret or a permanent one. Nothing, even a casual conversation, seemed quite simple anymore.

Agnes walked in strutting, looking like a gypsy Cat. Silver jewelry hung from her neck, and matching paw and tail bands gleamed as she turned around in the middle of the floor, modeling for her audience.

"How do you like them?" she purred. "I commissioned them with my latest paycheck. Shall I do a floor show?" Agnes danced sideways with little syncopated steps that sent Hannah into giggles. Even Putney laughed under his breath before pronouncing, "Not very practical for our work, is it?"

"Absolutely practical!" sang Agnes. "For my finale I will whip off my jewelry and merge with the necklace." She sat down. "Only it won't work, I think. I couldn't fit into it."

"At least you fit into it the ordinary way," said Hannah. "It looks good on you, too."

Agnes nodded her thanks to Hannah, then slipped out of the jewelry. "I suppose you should hear about our work these last two weeks," she said. "We've set up a graduated series of merged objects, varying in size and density. We're beginning to see distinct patterns in our ability to merge with them that should help us to reproduce the formula, eventually."

"I suppose you'll need me to supply the human element now?" asked Hannah.

"Oh, yes," Agnes answered. "And you can help get the shape-complexity experiments off the ground, too. They should come next."

"What about Margo Krupp? Has she come back? Have you seen her?"

"Yes and no," said Putney. "After that last gruesome visit, Agnes decided to be the one to make the next move. She wrote a letter to Doctor Krupp."

Agnes stood up. "I wrote it in big letters and pinned it conspicuously on my bedroom wall. Then we stayed clear of there for a while. I had a feeling she'd be back to see if we had followed her orders and given up working on merging. We know she read the note because we found it crumpled up on the floor later that day.

"It went like this: 'Come to us in peace. Let us speak openly in the name of Science. We hold all your secrets to our hearts. We need you.'"

"Perhaps too poetic," said Putney, with a hint of disapproval, "but certainly placating."

"Soothing the savage breast, I'd say," Agnes explained.

"I still don't understand why she wants us to stop," said Hannah. "I'm sure she was trying to warn us."

Agnes sat up straight and curled her tail around her paws. "There are only two ways to find that out: by continuing to work on merging or by hearing from Margo Krupp."

"Why does she seem so angry with us?"

"I wish I knew that. If you're right about her wanting to warn us, then what seems like anger to us may in fact be fear and concern."

"She should have come and told us, then. And taken her notes back. They were hers; all she had to do was ask for them."

"It's too late for that," said Putney.

"She must have wanted you to learn about merging once. She did give you the notes."

Agnes hunkered down, looking like a great ball of long fur. "That's what is so mysterious to me," she said. Her tail swung out low from her body and swished from side to side. "Margo's actions are full of contradictions. She willed me the notes, then destroyed them. She trusted me with a vital secret. But now she's setting fires in my apartment. And yet, two weeks have passed and she's made no further move to stop us from working. It's as if there were two different people in one body. I'm afraid Margo's gone at least a little bit mad."

Hannah shuddered involuntarily. She had felt like two different people herself many times in recent weeks. It had not been a pleasant feeling at all. Could merging make a person go mad? Or did you have to be a little bit mad in the first place to get as strange as Margo Krupp? What was madness anyway?

Hannah certainly didn't feel crazy right then. But maybe she had been a little crazy in the elevator and up on the rooftop. Or even that first time inside Agnes' wall. The old fear crept slowly, uncontrollably back. And a new idea was taking root.

"Could she be crazy," said Hannah slowly, "because she merges so much? I think a person could be. Sort of the way some people can get stranger and stranger from using certain drugs." She turned to Agnes.

"You knew Doctor Krupp before she started merging, Agnes. She wasn't really crazy then. Was she?"

Agnes and Putney looked at her, round-eyed. "Well, Hannah," Putney said at last, "you're human, and you know what a human feels like when she merges. Maybe you're on the right track."

"It doesn't wash for me," said Agnes brusquely. "After all, how could even dozens of mergings have such a devastating effect on a person? We're talking about an experience that lasts only a few minutes."

Hannah was shaking her head slowly. She tried to put her thoughts into words. "Maybe it *doesn't* last for only a few minutes, though. Maybe she merges for hours, even for days."

"Impossible," said Agnes.

Hannah looked at her. "How do you know?" she said.

"It's true," answered Agnes. "I don't know. I suppose anything is possible. I wouldn't doubt that Margo has a tremendous talent for merging, considering her extrasensory abilities, not to mention the time and energy she must have spent developing her skills."

Agnes stood up and began pacing. "But how, how, how can she stay inside something for a long time—live inside an object? Body functions can't just stop indefinitely, not without careful external controls. At least, I don't think they can. Merging may put the body into a state of suspended animation—but it's a totally different kind from the one produced in the controlled laboratory environment where we know suspended animation works over long periods."

"It's an astounding idea," said Putney. "Why would she spend so much time merging, anyway?"

"I think I know," said Hannah. "Merging is wonderful for a human. It's fantastic. It makes you feel things that you never felt, things that you didn't think you *could* ever feel."

Agnes turned and paced back to Hannah. "Imagine!" she cried. "Margo may be living in some object, perhaps in an altered state of mind, hidden away from everything." She stood and looked at the others. "But how could a person survive physically in such a state?"

"That may be the most important question we could raise about merging," said Putney excitedly. "Just how long can anyone survive in the merged state?" He rubbed his ear over and over. "It makes our other questions seem small and unimportant beside it."

"It seems to me," said Agnes, "that if our guess is correct about what Margo Krupp is doing . . . we have a marvelous resource for learning about this problem."

"Not Krupp?!" said Putney, his eyes wide.

"Of course, Krupp," said Agnes. "She's the expert, the master. We must start trying to reach out to her so she can help us with this. Who knows? We may even get her to start putting the notes together again with us."

"Now *you're* the one who is mad," said Putney. "Krupp will never agree. She wants us out of merging altogether."

Agnes' eyes glowed bright. "We will win back her trust. Convince her she's wrong. Then she'll work with us."

🌀 12 🌀

At first, the moon's cool rays seemed abruptly to be burning hot. Then, as she rose toward consciousness, Hannah realized the burning was within her, a psychic message searing her inside but coming from without. She was lying on the living-room floor, and as she opened her eyes, she saw a human figure standing by the window.

Blackened by the moonlight behind it, the figure first seemed like nothing but a deep shadow. The still silhouette made Hannah think of a statue, a Greek statue, with its head rising above the folds of a long, draped cloth. The figure moved then, turning slightly and stepping to the side so that the light now fell on a face, a face like none that Hannah had ever seen before.

Her hair was dark and was pulled back and lay in a heap on her head. It framed deep eyes and heavy dark eyebrows. A long, flaring nose drew Hannah's eyes down toward the figure's full but strangely hard mouth. In spite of the cold light, Hannah felt there must be color in this person's cheeks. It was a large face, almost a caricature of a face, and it looked down on Hannah from a long way away.

"Child," said a deep, tired voice. "You are only a child."

Hannah sat up. She saw now that this shadow had draped herself in the blanket discarded by Hannah during the night. Of course! she thought. She must have been naked.

Before Hannah could think of something to say, the figure spoke again.

"I understand," said the deep voice. "I know why you are continuing with the work. But you especially—a child—must stop. Wasn't my warning sufficient?"

Hannah opened her mouth, but the other voice went on without waiting.

"I did wish to frighten you. Yes, to make you afraid. Not of me, but of merging." A long shuddering sigh emerged from the shadows. The face that shone in the moonlight suddenly grew contorted. Her eyes became wide and her jaw tightened, but only for a moment.

"So, you don't understand at all. You think I'm just mad. Forgive me if I read your mind—I seem to have forgotten conventions of courtesy. But *must* I explain it all to you?

"You are wrong to continue," the figure said. "Merging is a terrible thing!" Her face went rigid with emotion. On that face, Hannah saw a kind of pain she had never known. Then, suddenly, it fell from the figure like a dropped cloth—and the face was dull, blank, tired.

"I will leave now. What more can I say? Nothing—or everything. I cannot stay." The figure turned to go.

"Wait," cried Hannah. "We need you. Merging *isn't* terrible. It's too wonderful to be terrible. And there is so much we need to learn. Please stay. Teach us and be with us. Please. . . ."

"I go," said the voice. "I will come again if I can, to tell you why you must stop."

The blanket fell away, and in the same movement the unclothed women seemed to melt into the wall behind her.

Hannah was alone now. Moonlight filled the room as she began to shiver. She rose and pulled the blanket around her, clutching it tightly. Hannah sat for a long time by the window, looking out, away from the room where Margo Krupp had been.

Sunlight at last came to the living room. Hannah was asleep, huddled by the window. She opened her eyes painfully and saw Putney atop the exercise-climber, poised like a jungle cat over unsuspecting prey. He sprang from the climber, arching gracefully, and landed with the mild, dull thump of padded paws hitting carpeting. Then he calmly turned and headed back to the climber to sharpen his claws.

Had she not been bursting with news, Hannah would have enjoyed watching this rare sight of the dawn exercise of a Cat. She sat up and said Putney's name in a whisper so as to break his concentration gently.

Putney's head swiveled round in a split second. He saw Hannah and instantly composed himself in a proper greeting stance.

"Good morning," he said. "This is quite early for you, isn't it?"

"I didn't sleep much at all last night. I couldn't. Margo Krupp was here."

"Margo Krupp! When? What happened? Did you actually see her?"

"I did see her."

"Did I hear the name *Margo Krupp*?" Agnes came in. She walked over to Hannah and peered into her face. "Did my letter work? Is she going to start helping us?"

"I don't think so," said Hannah.

"But didn't you tell her we need her to work with us?" Agnes asked.

"Yes, I did. But I don't think she listened. Agnes, Margo Krupp wasn't the way I thought she'd be. She was very clear about what she wanted; she didn't shout or do anything really crazy. She wants us to stop because she thinks merging is dangerous."

"Sure, it's dangerous," said Agnes. "We know it is. It's a great unknown."

"That's not what she means, though," protested Hannah. "I think . . . it's not a great unknown to Doctor Krupp. She said it was terrible. She wants to *protect* us from it. I'm sure she won't help us keep working."

Agnes sat down, looking suddenly tired. "Well," she said, "we're back where we started—all on our own, without Margo, even without her notes."

"There's *one* thing I think we can expect from her," said Hannah. "She'll be back, to explain why we can't go on."

"Why didn't she explain it last night?" Putney asked.

Hannah wrinkled her brow, puzzling out her memory of the midnight visit. "It was almost as if something were pulling her away. She left in a hurry, like she couldn't stand to be here any longer."

"Why?" asked Agnes.

There was no one to answer her. "I'm tired," said Hannah.

Agnes got up. "Come," she said. "You can sleep in the bedroom."

When she woke up, it was a relief, in a way, to find that most of the day had gone by. Pleasant smells floated in to Hannah from the kitchen, but she refused to be lured. She got up and started searching around for her belongings.

Agnes was in the kitchen, pressing buttons to adjust the temperature and moisture levels in the oven. She turned toward Hannah and noticed the backpack already slung over her shoulders.

"Ah, that's right. You must get home tonight. Are we still set then for Wednesday?"

Hannah nodded.

"It's too bad you can't continue to stay with us. Having you sleep here allows us to make the most of our time and be more flexible with it, too."

"There will be some nights I can stay, I suppose, if I check with my parents." But she was thinking of the chill of the night before and of her own warm, rose-colored bedroom.

"I'll be back as early as I can on Wednesday," she told Agnes. She left feeling as confused as ever. Now the tables seemed to have turned again—home was secure and Agnes' apartment a frightening place.

Hannah heard piano music coming through the door in great gusts and waves as she quietly turned the key. She saw her mother sitting in the Pit, apparently lost in listening to her father's playing. Her mother turned slightly and raised a finger to her mouth in a silencing gesture. Hannah slipped through the living-dining room and closed the door to her own room behind her.

Her room *was* peaceful. Its furnishings sat predictably, welcoming Hannah, basking in her satisfied gaze. Margo Krupp might once have followed Hannah here, but she could never upset her room's order, its Hannahness.

Not that it would be all that orderly to anyone else's gaze; a parade of years of memento collecting marched across the upper shelf of her desk, bookcase, and dresser, and half her clothes hung tiredly on six huge pegs. Her pictures of writers and singers were neatly framed and dusted, but they covered nearly every available inch of wall space. Only the deep rose-colored curtains against the window provided an undistracting place to rest the eye.

Hannah flopped facedown on her bed and lay there, thinking very little. When the smells of dinner reminded her of the meals she had missed that day, she rolled to a stand, pushed back her hair, and went to join her parents.

Her father was just getting up from the piano when Hannah entered.

"Our wayward Hannah is back for the summer now," he said, crossing the room to greet her. "I hardly saw you when you first returned on Friday."

Hannah kissed him. "That wasn't all my fault, Father. You were in the city rehearsing."

Her father shrugged. "That is the way it is with us," he said. "More and more so as you grow up. Fortunately, your mother is already grown—I see about as little of her now as I did ten years ago."

From the Pit, Hannah's mother laughed aloud. "With varying amounts of complaint from me, depending on how much you are needed at home."

"Be glad I don't work in some faraway office every day, my dear," said Hannah's father in a tone that clearly finished the subject.

"Doctor Shulevitz is coming at nine o'clock tomorrow for my lesson, isn't he?" Hannah asked as they sat down to dinner.

"Ivan promised me that," said her father, turning his attention to his plate. "And he is never late."

Hannah nodded and started to eat. Potato sausage and fruit stew had never tasted so good before.

"Your project with the Brancusis," said Hannah's mother, "is it something you can tell us more about, now that, well . . . now that you've been at it for some time?" Her head was bent over her plate.

Hannah stopped chewing. This again? she thought.

As if to smooth an uncomfortable scene, her mother added, "You know you have our approval for this, or we would not have let you go. Whether you tell us or not, you may continue with the plans you have made for the summer."

This was clearly a subject which had been discussed in Hannah's absence. But how could she blame her parents for wanting to know more? She had, more or less by accident, sheltered them from the difficulties of the last few weeks—she had seen so little of them throughout that time. But there was no hiding from them the importance of those meetings with the Brancusis.

Hannah put her fork down and folded her napkin. Her parents were quiet, looking at her. "It is a great scientific discovery, a mystery," she said at last. "And I am helping to unravel it. I and the Brancusis."

"Alone?" her mother asked.

"Well, almost. I don't have the freedom to tell you anything else for a while. I hope I can soon."

Her mother leaned toward her. "Is it dangerous, Hannah?"

"Not in any way that you are afraid it might be." She would never tell them just how frightening it all had been.

From across the table, her father spoke. "Our young daughter is growing up." He looked at Hannah in a way she could not understand.

Dr. Shulevitz perched over the piano, his delicate fingers making small birdlike movements as he demonstrated a technique to Hannah. She sat beside him, half listening and learning, half thinking what a strange man her piano teacher was.

Dr. Shulevitz turned toward Hannah and peered out through spectacles as thick as glass bottoms. "Do you see how loose my hand is, my entire arm? The power comes from that—relaxation and the force of the back, arm, and fingers." He stood up. "Now you try," he told Hannah. "Don't worry about what notes your fingers play for now. Just let them fall onto the keys with total relaxation."

Hannah centered herself at the piano and dropped her fingers onto the keyboard. She winced at the odd jumble of notes it produced, but her teacher's voice made her jump immediately.

"No! That is not relaxed. You are too afraid of hurting the piano. Now *fall* this time and don't worry about breaking the keys. Pianos are very, very strong."

It was true; she had been holding back and keeping her arm tight. So Hannah banged down on the piano. Again and again she hit it, with one hand, with both, as Dr. Shulevitz prompted her. Slowly she began to feel the looseness he had told her about, through her arms and shoulders. She smiled, knowing she was understanding.

"Good! Good! Now apply some pressure to the keys with the tips of your fingers. Keep the arm relaxed. You're tightening again. Get into those notes, without losing the looseness. That's it, keep going. Now, there is true force. . . ."

Suddenly Hannah heard the full, resounding tones she was making. It shocked her to realize she could learn this so quickly. She smiled as she let her fingers fall into the keyboard. Then, suddenly, she was laughing, laughing at a private joke. It had to do with falling a little too far into the keys. She wondered if she could do it and what the look on Dr. Shulevitz's face might be if her fingers disappeared into the piano.

"Hannah, why are you laughing like that?" The teacher's hands fumbled for hers and held them. He looked with concern at Hannah until she was able to calm down.

"Oh, I'm sorry," she told him. "I just thought of something. Something funny."

Her teacher let go of Hannah's hands and straightened up at the piano. He looked at his watch. "Yes . . . well. It's time to stop. I think you have done quite well. Just continue this week with the exercises I gave you. Since you can already read notes from your lessons a few years back, we can begin with some real music next week." He stood up and flattened his thin, black hair down with his palm. "Plan to practice at least one hour each day. You may take one day off during the week."

Hannah nodded, holding back a sigh as she thought of the work that was to come. She hoped fervently that she would like playing the piano as much as she had thought she would. Then at least there would be some reward for her labors.

The phone rang just as she closed the door behind Dr. Shulevitz. "Yes Agnes, just a moment," she heard her father say from the Pit. She felt a thin trickle of fear run through her.

She walked up to the receiver grid. "Hi, Agnes. What's up?"

"We have a visitor today," said Agnes, her voice strangely flat. "She wants to speak with you, in person."

Hannah looked at her father waiting nearby, who quickly glanced about the room. "The telephone won't do, I suppose."

"I would think not," Agnes answered. "Our guest will not speak with anyone else but you, by the way. Can you come?"

She wanted to shout "No!" into the receiver grid

and make Agnes go away. "I haven't been home one day, Agnes," she said into the phone. "My parents aren't ever going to see me."

She felt her father's hand on her arm. "Go," he said quietly. "Go and come back when you can."

Hannah sighed. "I'm coming. Make your visitor stay till I get there."

"I'll do my very best." The phone clicked off. Hannah kissed her father and went to fill her backpack.

❧ 13 ☙

At first, it had seemed to happen fast—Hannah was ushered in by Agnes, her backpack was taken from her, then hurried words of support were whispered.

But now, in the quiet bedroom, moments stood still. Hannah faced Margo Krupp, draped in a bed sheet, sitting cross-legged against the far wall. She looked different from the last time, calmer, not suffering so much. Hannah felt as if she were being examined minutely and judged—for what, she had no inkling. She knew her mind was being read and that she had no power to stop it. It was not a good feeling.

Margo Krupp spoke: "I have come, one final time,

to tell you why you must stop this work. When I am through, you will understand.

"What could possibly stop you? You think. . . . Ah, you are more strong-willed than I gave you credit for. You remind me of myself at your age: force, determination, and more force.

"But now, you must listen—and do not expect answers to your questions. I cannot spend much time here."

Hannah sat down opposite Margo Krupp. She waited for the woman to speak again.

"I have always believed," she began, "that a person must be only what she wants to be. The world fights differences, people hate strangeness. But, if you *are* different, if you have a heart's desire that does not fall neatly into someone else's plan for you, follow your heart. I would rather be here, on the precipice of time, than be molded into a shape my heart found uncomfortable. I have always fought the ease of going gentle into some good night.

"Deep inside me, I always knew about merging. It was a dream, but I needed to make it come true. I believed in it, and I made it work.

"When I first unlocked those doors that led to merging, it was all triumph, exhilaration! There could be no greater act in my life. I practiced it, worked on it, and it became my life. I did not notice its fingers slowly reaching out to grasp me. I only wanted more.

"You have had that feeling, I know it. I don't even have to read your thoughts; I can see it written on your face. You have experienced the beauty of being without form and the pull of this great feeling. But it grows. It doesn't stop!

"Caught in that feeling, I began to think: Could there be greater, more profound ways to merge? I decided that there was a horizon yet to reach. And then I found it.

"What would it be like to *become* a thing? To merge with some great machine that could take me places no living person had ever been before. I would travel in the universe of the inanimate—as a member of that universe. Suddenly the idea of merging for only a few moments was like a poor reflection of the real beauty, like an unfinished work of art.

"That is why I took the journey into space. I carefully planned the 'accident' that was to allow me to disappear forever. The poor fools in my ship believed they had left me adrift in the cosmos.

"But I had merged with my beautiful ship. I had left this pitiful, inept body behind to share my life with a ship, to feel its movements through space and its intricate, perfect workings. To know the white heat of its engines, and its speed, and the frigid cold of its shell as it carved through the vastness of black space.

"No doubt there are those who would have tried to stop me, to 'save' me or perhaps even to save the ship from me. But I did not care to be saved. I did what I had to do.

"My ship has been resting now, for a number of weeks. I rested too, with its body as my own. And then I discovered the hand that had wound its fingers tightly around me.

"I left the ship one day, to find out what it would be like to have a human body once again. I discovered I could not bear it; I hurried back. It occurred to me that, for the first time in my life, I was not in complete control, that something else determined my actions.

"I fought it, of course. I emerged from the ship again and again, defying the pull of it.

"But the fight weakened me. Each time I left the ship, it became harder to do. I realized that I was trapped.

"Never have I been in despair before; never have I let myself fall that far. But this time, I had reached the black bottom, where no one should ever go. And then, I started up. I saw that I was caught, but that I might fight with whatever was left of me. The one thing I could do, however hard it might be, was to see to it that the hand that gripped me could not reach anyone else. With all the force left in me, I came to you and did what had to be done. I burned the records of my work. I thought: I have destroyed my triumph, a beautiful thing, a terrible enemy of life.

"Now, there is only you, Hannah, and the two Cats. I have watched all of you. I do not fear for Agnes and Putney; they seem unaffected. I think that Cats cannot experience the real beauty—and the terror—of merging. But you, a human, can—and have.

126

"You could go on without the notes, and without me. But you will become like me, and if you reveal our secret to the world, others will follow."

Margo Krupp drew a long, uneven breath. "I cannot stay much longer," she said. "My will is weakening with every moment. But I must say one more thing.

"My story is not finished. There is yet another horizon for me—the final one. When I reach it, I will not be able to return. That is a thing of which I am sure. I am equally certain that it will be the most beautiful and terrible of all acts, more than any person can bear. Yet I must do it. I am a seeker of horizons, and I am set on a course from which I cannot diverge."

Margo Krupp rose. "Good-bye, child. I go now to join my ship, to gather strength for my last flight."

She cast away the sheet and slipped into the wall.

Hannah rushed into the living room, stumbling in her speed. Putney and Agnes hurried to her.

"She's going to kill herself!" she said in a strange, high voice. "I think she's going to kill herself."

"We must try to stop her," said Agnes. "Do you know where she's going?"

"The ship!" Hannah shouted. "Where is her ship?"

"What ship?" asked Putney.

"The last one she was on. She's been living in it, merged with it all this time. She's gone back there."

"Quick!" said Agnes. "I'll get the docking tables of the spaceships." She hurried to the telephone and pressed a long series of buttons. There was a seemingly endless wait until a mechanical voice spoke.

"Transportation Information, Interplanetary Division. May I help you?"

Agnes spoke into the phone. "Docking-orders information request: Earth-moon shuttle . . . um . . . *Mercury VII*."

There was another wait. Then the voice said, "Southern Terminal, Dock 86. Thank you." Agnes punched the Off button and the three of them hurried to the door.

They took the monorail. Minutes sped by as they wondered how fast Margo Krupp could travel and if she would be where they hoped she was.

The monorail stopped at the Southern Terminal Station. They leaped onto the ped belt that carried people to the terminal and darted around other passengers as the belt silently moved everyone forward.

In the terminal they ran the long corridor to Dock 86. A guard stood at the door to the huge hangar that held the ship.

"Sorry," he said, "this dock is closed to the public. The ship has no scheduled flights until Monday."

"I am Doctor Brancusi," said Agnes breathlessly. "I have special clearance from the government. I'm investigating the death of Doctor Krupp."

The guard eyed them suspiciously. "Papers? Do you have papers and identification?"

"This is an emergency," pleaded Agnes. "If we are not out in ten minutes, you may call the police. We *must* be let in."

"Highly irregular," said the guard, but he must have sensed the urgency of Agnes' request. "I will call the police in *five* minutes, not ten." He opened the door to the hangar. "Go in quickly," he whispered.

The ship towered before them, silver and immense.

"How are we to know if she's there?" asked Putney. "How do we get her out?"

Agnes thought a moment. "One of us must go in after her. There is no other way."

"Go in after her? How?" said Hannah. "Who?" She was frightened beyond thinking, but the answer seemed obvious.

Agnes looked at her. "No, Hannah. I know why you think it has to be you, but I rather feel it *can't* be you."

"Why?" asked Hannah. "She won't even talk to you. How could you get her to come out?"

"I *will* get her to come out," Agnes replied. "I must. The risk is simply too great for you. I cannot bear that responsibility."

Hannah simply nodded. She and Putney watched Agnes approach the ship calmly. They saw her merge with it and then they waited. Moments ticked by. They could hear the sounds of the terminal, the roar of engines being started somewhere far off. Inside the hangar there was only silence, as things happened beyond the imaginings of most people.

Putney's tail flicked from side to side. "What can be taking so long? What is happening in there?"

Suddenly Agnes burst from the ship's side. She turned around as Margo Krupp followed her out, stepping with dignity.

"Back, all of you!" Margo Krupp commanded.

"We must speak with you," said Agnes.

"Back!" the other shouted. Agnes took faltering backward steps.

"Why do you come here now? Why do you disturb my final meditations?"

"Because we don't want them to *be* your final meditations," said Agnes. "You must not destroy yourself."

"Destroy myself? I am not going to destroy myself. I am going to do the exact, perfect opposite of it. I am not ending my life; I am expanding it, beyond any power known on earth." She looked at the three of them with great sadness. "You don't understand, do you? I am about to join the universe in its celebration of life."

A glimmering began in Hannah's mind. It was an idea that was almost beyond imagining. "Wait," she called. "You can't leave. I *do* understand. But we can't just pretend you never made your discovery. It's too important to forget. We'll help you fight. You can continue your work."

Margo Krupp drew herself up and spoke quietly. "I shall continue it. Forever. My work will never end and my life will never end. Good-bye."

She closed her eyes. And, as the three of them stood there, a throbbing began in the air, a pulsing energy that came from the woman standing before them.

A fine, white radiance filled the hangar as slowly, the figure of Margo Krupp grew dimmer and dimmer. The throbbing became sound—a high humming pitch that increased in volume. And then the figure of Margo Krupp, as if exploding slowly, came apart in a billion pieces that scattered in unending paths.

The humming and the whiteness stopped. There was no one in the hangar except two Cats and a girl.

Full of fear, Hannah turned to Agnes.

"She has merged," said Agnes, "with the universe. She is one with everything."

There was no need for the guard to call the police. They left the hangar in silence and rode the ped belt and monorail back, each of them trying to find the pieces of the puzzle, to make them fit together.

As the Bissell Street Station drew near, Hannah spoke to the Cats.

"I'd like to go home now," she told them. They nodded and stood up. "We'll see you—tomorrow?" asked Putney.

"All right," said Hannah. "I'll get my backpack then." She remained on the monorail and watched them go.

Where was Margo Krupp? She *couldn't* have done what Agnes said she did. That would mean she was everywhere, even in the monorail car Hannah was riding. Even in *her*, Hannah. She couldn't be. She was gone forever from anything normal people could call life. Yet *she was not dead either*.

It was too much to think about, and it left her feeling exhausted and horribly, deeply sad.

Although it was only midday, Hannah went straight to bed when she got home, and fell into a sound sleep.

She didn't wake up until stars lit her room and the rest of the house was quiet. She lay in bed, thinking for hours. At dawn, she slept again.

⊙14⊙

It was morning. Someone was knocking on Hannah's door.

"I have breakfast for you," said her mother from the doorway. "Do you want to get up now, Hannah?"

Hannah sat up in bed. "I'll be there in a minute," she called, and went to get ready.

"Is it over?" her mother asked when Hannah came down to the Pit.

Hannah smiled a little, surprised that it could show. "It's over," she said.

Her mother smiled too. "Back to ordinary old piano lessons and a nice, relaxing summer."

"Yes, I guess so. I'm going to see the Brancusis today, though. One more time."

Agnes and Putney were waiting for her. "Come and sit down," said Agnes. "We have some things to talk about."

Hannah sat down and took a sip of the tea Agnes had poured for her.

Putney spoke first. "Agnes and I have decided that it is time to choose what happens to the experiments and the reconstruction of the notes. Do we tell anyone about them or forget the whole thing? We want to let you help us. You know about merging in a different way than we do."

Hannah took a deep breath. "I was hoping," she told them, "that you would ask me. Because I have decided some things about merging on my own." She took another long breath and said, "I think you should go on. And I think you should tell the world."

Agnes looked at Putney, then back to Hannah. "I am glad. Will you tell us why?"

"I was right about merging," said Hannah. "It was like a terrible addiction for Margo Krupp. It killed her, or at least it destroyed her body. But maybe it won't destroy everyone. Doctor Krupp herself said she wasn't worried about what it could do to Cats. She also said not to ever let someone keep you from doing what's really important to you. If merging is important to the two of you, then I suppose even

Margo Krupp would have to think twice about making you stop doing it."

"Merging seems more dangerous than ever," said Agnes, "but it is very, very important to me. Margo Krupp gave me one of the great discoveries of all time —Putney and I, in turn, will give it to the scientific community and the world. I accept your decision."

"Agnes? Where is Margo Krupp?" asked Hannah.

"I don't know. But, even if she is alive somewhere, she has still destroyed herself as far as I am concerned, because she cannot be human anymore, or live the way humans do."

Hannah was filled with sadness for a person she hardly knew. "She *wasn't* mad, was she?"

"No," said Putney, "she wasn't mad. But she wasn't like other people, either. It was as if she had a looking glass; she saw the world through a mirror that made it appear different. She kept looking in that mirror and after a while, I suppose, the reflection seemed more real than reality. And what was real seemed pale, unsatisfying. She still saw the real world—our world—but I think it just ceased to have much meaning for her."

"And then," said Agnes, "she stepped into that looking glass world and disappeared."

"But . . ." Hannah faltered, "was it merging that did it, or was it Margo Krupp?"

There was no answer from the Cats. They sat, looking lost in thought.

"I'm not going to work on this anymore," said Hannah after a while.

"Because of the looking glass?" Agnes asked.

"No, because of what Margo Krupp said, about living your own life. I liked being brave, in a way. It made me feel more like me than when I was just plodding along, being good old reliable, obedient Hannah. But, if I'm going to be brave, I want to choose where and how. And this is not the place, now is not the time." Hannah stood up.

"You go on with the experiments. There are lots of other people who can help. Better people than me, for this kind of thing."

Agnes nodded. "I like that. And you're right. It is time to find others. No more makeshift laboratories, no more secrecy."

"What will you do now?" asked Putney.

Hannah smiled. "I have catching up to do. Being a kid takes a lot of energy."